BOOKS BY LESLIE FEAR

ATTICUS

WITH C.D. HUSSEY

VILLERE HOUSE
BAYOU GRISE: SINS OF SANITE

ATTICUS

LESLIE FEAR

http://lesliefear.blogspot.com

ACKNOWLEDGEMENTS:

To my betas: Paige Weaver, Sarah Phelps, Beth Rustenhaven, Stephenie Thomas, Laura Wilson, Vanessa Proehl, Tami Fairley, Chelcie Dacon and Tashia Brandenburg. Thank you for your honesty, your patience and your time. Your opinions were like gold and I am so grateful for each and every one of you.

To all the readers and bloggers: I am honored and thrilled to share my first solo book with you and I hope you enjoy it as much as I loved writing it.

To Beth Rustenhaven, my fellow TIB girl and pimp: Your never-ending support and willingness to help in any way with blog tours, cover reveals, even making posters and bookmarks has been incredible and saying, "thank you" just isn't enough. I love ya, chick.

To Paige Weaver: Thank you for brainstorming with me through several lunches, not to mention the copious amounts of back and forth texts. You were a beacon of light when I needed guidance and reassurance and I adore you.

To Erin Roth, my editor: You kicked my behind when I needed it and made me a better writer because of it. Thank you for your professionalism and dedication.

To Sarah Phelps, my proofreader: Your eagle eye amazes me! Thank you for your incredible support and for always having such a generous heart.

And lastly, to my lovely husband, Randy: Without you this book wouldn't have been written. You are my world, my truest friend and my biggest supporter. I cherish you, I thank you...and I love you all the way to the barn and back...forever.

PROLOGUE

THEY COME UNINVITED and unwanted. The barriers meant to keep them out have been broken, allowing their unscrupulous thoughts and desires to stay hidden from the outside world. They are thieves, invading in the cloak of night, scavenging a hiding place for their foul intentions. I am sickened, yet I deeply desire what they have, wishing I could be cherished in the same way.

They know not of my existence. Only rumors fuel their curiosity to investigate, ravaging what was once a grand house. Now it is merely a shell of what it was—full of life, fine art, and furniture. But all of that is no more and it pierces the same knife through my heart as jealousy of what I can never have begins to ravage my soul.

"C'mon, Nick, don't be such a pussy."

"Screw you, Paul, you're the one who's scared of this place."

"Jesus, keep your voices down."

"Yeah, listen to your mother—I mean, Brad."

"Just get in here, asshole."

"Nick, did you bring a light?"

"Yeah, hang on."

"Holy shit, get a load of that spider web. Oh, sorry, Paul, did that scare you?"

"Yeah, you're fucking hilarious, Nick."

"Brad, toss me a beer."

"Yeah, toss me one, too."

"Jesus! What the hell is this?"

"It's free. Give it back if you're not gonna drink it."

"No, I like cold piss."

"Yeah, you would."

"Shit, it's cold in here."

"It's September, Paul. It's supposed to be cold."

"Not this cold."

"Jesus, are you gonna pussy-out every time we come here?"

"Shut up, Nick."

"No, he's right, Nick, it's fucking cold in here."

"Ahh, do you want me to get you a blankie, Brad?"

"Asshole."

"Jesus, did you hear that?"

"Looky there, Paul lasted a full five minutes before he grew a pussy."

"Did you seriously not hear that?"

"Yeah, I heard it. But this house is old and probably rat-infested. Chill the fuck out."

"There it is again."

"I know you heard that, Nick."

"Sounded like it came from upstairs."

"That's impossible. No one's here."

"Then what could slam a door, Brad?"

"I don't know. There's gotta be air coming in."

"Shhh! Wait…"

"What the hell is that?"

"Sounds like whispering?"

"Sounds more like a conversation."

"Yeah, but from where?"

"Upstairs?"

"No, it came from the hallway."

"Hold up. Maybe someone's playing a joke on us."

"Paul, did you tell anyone where you were going?"

"Why the fuck would I tell anyone?"

"Maybe because you're a pussy?"

"Shut up, you two. Nick, come with me. Paul, stay here until we get back."

"I'm not staying here alone!"

"See? He's a pussy."

"Fuck you…"

"Jesus, keep your voices down! Nick, just take Paul outside—and make sure no one's fucking with us. I'll look upstairs and meet you back here in a few."

"We only have one flashlight."

"You guys take it. I have matches somewhere."

"Boy Scout Brad has arrived—should we synchronize our watches?"

"Just go before I change my mind and kick both your asses."

"Oh wow, now he's Ninja Brad."

"Hey, you got a better idea, I'm all ears."

"Fine. C'mon, Pussy—I mean, Paul."

"Call me that again. I dare ya."

"Pussy."

"Shit, are you kidding me? Break it up! Paul, give me the fucking flashlight before you kill somebody."

"He started it!"

"And you're a pussy!"

"Jesus, grow up!"

"Holy shit!"

"What was that?"

"I don't know, but it definitely came from inside this room!"

"Let's get out of here!"

CHAPTER ONE

LILBURN, GEORGIA – 1992

~~CANDICE~~

I N A MANNER of minutes, I'll be walking into my fourth high school and everyone will be staring at the new girl. We've moved so many times in the past three years, I'm nauseated before I even leave this crappy apartment. This time, we've landed in the middle of small town Georgia because Mom ran out of money and needs a job. Again.

Thank God this is my last year in high school.

"Candice!" Mom screams from downstairs. "Where's my tip money?" The bite in her voice practically slaps me in the face.

Mom's already pissed and it's only seven thirty in the morning. That might be a new record. She must have forgotten where she hid it again, but I can't tell her that or even admit that I can usually find it within minutes.

I'm pretty sure I know why she's been more on edge than normal. Every penny she had saved was eaten up by having to pay our first and last month's rent and now we're living on her leftover tips.

Clearly, I need to be more careful because I *have* been hoarding some of it. Not much, just a few dollars here and there because living for days without tampons and shampoo finally sent me over the edge. I promised myself I would only do it once, but that didn't stick either. Sneaking money has become a dirty little habit, but one I only do when she's passed out. Which is often. I made a joke with myself (as if it excuses my bad behavior), calling them my "dirty dollars." I'm pretty sure she thinks stashing her money in an old Folgers can is a good idea. But all it does is make my life easier. I know how her mind works. Mom never puts a lot of thought into anything—she simply reacts.

I often wonder if Mom actually does know. She has to be smarter than to think certain bathroom items just magically appear but just thinking about it scares me way more than my first day of school.

I would love to tell her that she's destroyed my life and to go straight to hell. But I can't. I have no doubt she would slap the shit out of me if I did. So I go off on her in my mind instead. I've done it countless times.

Every morning Mom goes through an entire pack of cigarettes and every morning she sneaks shots of her favorite cheap whiskey. I'm convinced she thinks she's good at hiding her drinking, but she's *never* been good at it. The simple truth is, my stealing is the only way we can survive in her whiskey-fueled waste of a life.

"Did you hear me, little missy?" she yells, her tone demonstrating another level of pissed off.

I hate when she calls me that. It means she's about to explode. The alcohol has kicked in and the mean drunk has arrived. She's definitely gearing up for a fight.

"Yes, I heard you! And I don't know where your money is!" I lie, shouting a little louder than I should.

I don't have time to regret my words because I hear footsteps pounding up the stairs. In a matter of seconds she's standing next to me, ready to pounce. I am her prey. I need to cool her down or risk sporting a red handprint across my face on the first day of school.

"I'm sorry, Mom. I guess I'm a little nervous," I answer in the most toned down voice I can muster.

She yanks my wrist hard, sending shooting pain up my arm, but I don't dare move away.

"You raise your voice at me like that again, it'll take braces to sort out the bloody mess."

Her eyes are huge, almost pulsating, her face only inches from mine. She stumbles a little, no doubt from the whiskey, and takes a step forward, reeking of cigarette smoke. She knows I can't stand the smell; I know she's waiting for my reaction. If I show my utter disgust, it'll be the worst decision I make today. So I don't do anything. I know she can feel my revulsion and I'm pretty sure she knows I hate damn near everything about her.

We stand for what seems like hours—locked at the eyes—like we're in some kind of standoff. I flinch because she suddenly turns and stomps back down the stairs.

"I'm out of cigarettes," she growls over her shoulder, slamming the front door.

I don't say a word and have a new sense of urgency to get the hell out of here before she comes back.

Suddenly school doesn't seem quite so bad.

CHAPTER TWO

"WELCOME TO PARKVIEW High! I'm Mrs. Stephens," the overly enthusiastic counselor says, gesturing me into her office. Her periwinkle blue jumpsuit is my first clue that a '70s hippie wardrobe is alive and well in her closet. I don't think I've ever seen so many bracelets, ear piercings, or necklaces on one person before. Eccentric doesn't even cover it.

I smile back, even though I know it's not quite reaching my eyes, and take a seat anyway. I notice right away a large framed diploma from The University of Georgia hanging just above the credenza and what look like framed family photos neatly placed below. I close my eyes for a second and swallow.

Family.

Wouldn't *that* be nice?

Opening the manila envelope I handed her when I walked in, Mrs. Stephens takes out my transcripts and places them on her desk. She begins to look over them as if double-checking the contents. The constant popping sound she's making with her gum is annoying the crap out of me.

Seconds later, she glances up, like she knows I'm irritated, quickly taking the gum out of her mouth and placing it into a tissue. I'm instantly embarrassed for being annoyed but I don't know why. It's not like she can read my mind.

I'm a little distracted when she says, "Oh wow, I see you've been to a new high school every year for the past..." she pauses to calculate, "three years." She looks up at me. "Is your father in the military?"

I perk up when I hear the word "father" and hope my expression doesn't give away how ignorant she sounds.

Military.

I wish.

My father worked as everything from a used car salesman to a service department manager, but could never keep any job for long. One after the other, he'd get fired for not showing up, and looking back, it explains why my parents fought so much. Mom even kicked Dad out a few times, but he would eventually come back. Probably because he couldn't afford to live on his own and Mom didn't like being alone.

Most of the time, we had nothing but the money Mom brought in, but I can't help wondering if it was her fault that he left for good. When Mom found out he was having an affair with a younger, less demanding woman she went ballistic, filing divorce papers almost immediately. He tried to stop her, but her temper wouldn't allow it. She called the shots and she never let a day go by without reminding him of it.

I was thirteen, watching through the open crack of my bedroom door as they fought their last fight. I haven't seen or spoken to him since. That was five years ago and so many times I've wanted to scream, "Why didn't you fight for me?"

He's never been a fighter. He's always been a quitter. And tiny pieces of my soul are scattered everywhere because of it.

"No, my parents are divorced," I say, trying to hide the new bruise forming on my wrist.

The counselor's eyes pop back up at me from behind horn-rimmed glasses. Her head cocks to one side and again, it feels like she knows all my secrets. I'm suddenly uneasy, hoping I'm not that transparent.

"Oh, I see." Her smile practically drips of syrup as she takes off her glasses. "Okay, Miss Crawford. I think we have everything we need." She picks up a piece of paper and hands it to me. "Here's your schedule."

"Thanks." I take it, turning toward the door as I stuff it in my backpack. My mind is racing and I'm about to twist the knob when I hear her voice over my shoulder.

"Candice?"

"Yeah." I turn around, hoping she'll be quick. She's focused at me with a new look of concern.

"If you need anything, anything at all..." She pauses, as if wanting to say more. "I'm here to help."

Her sincere words punch me in the gut and it's all I can do to keep from falling apart right here in her office. Images begin popping up in my mind of the kind of mom she probably is. Loving, caring, kind.

So many things I don't have.

"Okay, thanks," I squeak out, darting out the door.

The second I step into the hallway I'm knocked on the side of the arm by a girl who isn't paying attention. She laughs as she walks by with her friend and I immediately feel invisible, lost in the sea of people rushing around me. I don't like crowded places. And after my chat with Mrs. Stephens, all I want to do is hide. I feel completely exposed, like I'm naked and everyone's eyes are on me, judging all my imperfections.

But I know I can't hide. I have to face this school, these people, these crowded hallways. Just like all the others. So I duck back in a corner, breathing in through my nose then slowly exhaling through my mouth. I do it two more times, telling myself to suck it up because sucking it up is what I do on a daily basis.

I'm still standing frozen in one spot, hoping my mini-panic attack will go away when I spot something familiar. 1117. My locker number. I only glanced at it when Mrs. Stephens handed me my schedule. I'm weird about numbers. I can remember them like a photograph in my head but I totally suck at math. This number also happens to be Dad's birthday. November seventeenth. I see it everywhere. I almost always happen to look at the clock and find that it's 11:17. And now it's my locker number. Maybe the universe enjoys screwing with me.

Luckily it's close enough not to dread the short walk over, and after I struggle to get the stupid thing to open, I throw in my backpack and pull out my crumpled schedule. First period is Geography, room 110. Silently, I thank God for small favors because I know where that is, too. I passed it when I was looking for the counselor's office.

CHAPTER THREE

After finding a seat in the back of the class, I can finally get a deep breath. I know the hardest part about being the new girl is the *being new* part, but my stomach still has some catching up to do. It's nothing new; I pretty much stay in a perpetual state of uneasiness thanks to the unpredictable world I live in. The first few weeks are always the worst though.

I manage to clear my head long enough to take a few notes in between the occasional stare from a guy next to me and again from a girl on my left. I swear it'd be easier if I just wore a freaking nametag saying, "I'm new, not an alien."

When the bell rings I bolt out of the room as quickly as I can. My only focus is to find my next class before I have to ask for help. I don't want favors and I don't want charity because nothing in my world is free. Everything is conditional. I thought by now I'd be used to the way we live but what I really do is fake it. Just like my mom. Most of the time I feel like I'm on autopilot, trudging through life with no direction, only hers.

Even so, this place is still better than being home. Even if that's fake, too.

The crowded hallway is making it impossible to see the room numbers and my stomach is back to its prickly self. Hoping to give it a minute or two to calm, I decide to find a restroom and spot my salvation just down the hall. Wedging my way through the crowds, I reach for the handle and pull, realizing within seconds that I just opened the men's door. I'm immediately pushed back, losing my balance and landing flat on my ass in the middle of the hallway. Everything feels like it happened in super slow motion until I notice a small gathering of students starting to surround me. I'm pretty sure not one of them is here to help. Laughter confirms it.

Shit.

"Whoa, you okay?" The tall guy who burst through the door has a surprised look on his face and immediately begins picking up the pencils, pens, and notebook paper scattered all over the floor. I look around, still a little dazed, and begin frantically stuffing everything I see in my backpack. I reach for the last pencil, but he grabs it before I can get to it then stands, reaching his hand out to me. I look up, leaping to my feet without taking it because on top of being completely humiliated, I'm trying my best to act unaffected by the sharp pain in my tailbone.

His face changes and for a moment he looks distracted. I turn away, pretending to read my schedule as he walks past me. He waves his hands, shooing away the now larger group of snickering onlookers. "Okay, everyone, show's over."

Everyone scrambles like they've been caught fighting in the hallways and I'm secretly grateful, pretending to read my schedule while trying to act oblivious. He turns around, walking straight for me, and I'm able to get a better look at him in my periphery. The confidence in his stride is impressive and I assume right then he must be some kind of leader. Maybe the student council president or the captain of the baseball team. He pauses next to me in his tight Levi's and un-tucked light blue Polo and cocks his head, as if to get a better look at my schedule.

"You sure you're okay?"

I glance up at him. "Yes, I'm fine," I lie, not only embarrassed as hell; I also have no clue where my next class is.

"Do you need help?" he asks as I turn away.

"I said I'm *fine*," I shoot over my shoulder, walking down the hallway without looking back.

He laughs and I stop immediately and turn around. His smile gets bigger when our eyes meet and I watch his lips reveal perfectly straight white teeth. "I saw your schedule. Chemistry is this way." Jerking his head to the right, he turns and starts walking, then glances back to see if I'm following—which I am.

"I could have found it on my own," I say a little abruptly, probably sending out a royal bitch vibe.

"You're welcome. It's the least I can do for knocking you down." His smile is back and I can tell he's amused by my little tantrum. "You can even sit next to me. I promise not to abuse you again."

He winks and I roll my eyes, pushing back the grin I think he already saw. I'm immediately pissed at myself because there's something about him I like. And the last thing I want is some random dude thinking I need help.

"Nope, I'm good. I'm pretty sure I can at least find a seat."

"I'm Brad Davis, by the way." He reaches out his hand and I take it because what else am I supposed to do?

"Um, Candice—Candice Crawford."

His warm hand feels amazing around my cool fingers, griping tightly but not too tight. He doesn't let go right away and my eyes go straight to his. He's still smiling but this time it's genuine, without the cockiness from before. Blood rushes to my face and I'm sure it's turned six shades of red. I'm not used to sincerity, not even a little bit. I drop his hand and step past him.

I learned my lesson a long time ago to keep a low profile. I can't allow anyone to get too close or find out my life is a complete disaster. I just want to graduate as soon as humanly possible. I'm not going to fall for the first guy who's nice to me. Even if he is totally my type. Tall, good-looking, and confident.

Shit.

I try to hide the deep breath I just took as I quickly scan the room for a seat. I probably shouldn't be surprised that the only one left is next to him.

How convenient.

Hearing him chuckle under his breath, I walk over and take the empty chair, half wondering if he planned it all along. I shake my head, finally cracking another smile I don't want to show. I'm mad at myself all over again for encouraging him.

A few seconds later, a man in a blue corduroy jacket sporting gray elbow patches walks through the door. I watch him stack papers, perfectly organizing them in a row, at his desk at the front of the room. Several minutes go by and he still hasn't spoken a word. I start to panic a little, thinking he's some kind of sadist about to hit us with a sneaky pop quiz on the first day of school. But, thankfully, he finally pulls out a spiral notebook and begins roll call.

Something catches the corner of my eye and I turn to see Brad leaning toward me.

"Hey," he says, whispering like it's a secret.

"Yeah?" I turn my head and watch his lips curl up then he looks down at my mouth.

"Let me know if you need any help finding the ladies' room."

CHAPTER FOUR

~~BRAD~~

I T WAS A stroke of sheer luck that the seat next to me was empty. And when Candice Crawford sat down, it was hard to keep my eyes off her.

She caught me by surprise and I felt like shit watching her fall outside the restroom. I instantly began picking up items tossed from her backpack and was curious when she didn't take my hand when I stood up. I wasn't expecting that kind of response. We stayed frozen in an awkward silence for a split second before she jumped to her feet, unaware I was still watching her. I didn't like how her face contorted and I knew without question she was in pain. I immediately got rid of the assholes doing nothing but laughing, yet somehow my small gesture wasn't enough. I wanted to do more, but when she looked up at me I couldn't think.

I offered my help when the bell rang because I was pretty sure she didn't know where her next class was either, but she turned me down. I couldn't help but laugh, even though she was a complete stranger to me; she was trying to be tough and do everything on her own. Her walls were up so I started to walk away but I had to look back. When I did, I caught another glimpse of her amazing blue eyes and the humiliation blanketing her face. Why it hit me in the gut like it did is still a mystery, but I wanted to help her and didn't feel obligated the second time. I needed to make the suffering behind those beautiful eyes go away. So I did the only thing I could think of. I teased her until she finally smiled. When she did, it was like the sun had squeezed its way out behind a deck of thick clouds.

CHAPTER FIVE

~~CANDICE~~

A LL DURING CHEMISTRY, I felt Brad's eyes on me and it seemed like forever before class was over. I wish I were like other, normal girls, excited to have the attention of an attractive guy. But I simply can't have him right now—not when my life is shit. My head won't allow it even though my heart doesn't understand. I've never had roots and I sure as hell don't think we'll stick around here long enough for them to grow.

I wait for most of the students to leave before I try to stand because I'm pretty sure I'll need a second. I have no doubt I'll look like I'm a hundred for the first few steps. The pain in my lower back isn't as bad as it was at the beginning of class, but the last thing I want is to draw attention to myself. I'll risk being tardy.

As I leave the room I see Brad standing outside the door and I make the mistake of looking up at him. His lips curl up and for a split second, I can't remember why I told myself to stay away from him.

"Need some help finding your next class?"

He comes up next to me like he's looking for my schedule but I can't react because I'm too busy staring at him, wondering why he's being so nice.

"You okay?" he asks, and I snap out of it and nod. He probably feels guilty for making me fall on my ass.

As if relieved, his face tightens up into another smile and I quickly realize that he didn't have to wait for me or offer any more help. It was an accident and I'm the one who made it happen, but he is making me question my own *no dating until college*, rule.

"Sucks to fall down on your first day," he says in a flirty way and grins, like he's giving me permission to laugh about it now.

I shake my head and can't help but smile back, fighting the urge to smack my own face because I don't want to like him this much.

Dammit.

"I'm an expert at making first impressions," I answer, a little breathless. He's standing so close that I can smell the soapy, masculine scent on his skin.

"Yeah," he says, looking me up and down. "I noticed."

~~

I end up having two more classes with Brad, which, thank God, limited the number of times I got lost since I refused to ask for help. Thankfully, this school isn't as big as the last one, so I should have it memorized pretty quickly.

After the last bell, I decide to skip going to my locker to avoid yet another avalanche of people blocking me from getting anywhere.

The instant I push on the double doors a strong breeze whips my hair in all directions and I reach over my neck to pull it to one side. I have to squint because the sun is so bright and I wish I had my cheap Dollar Store sunglasses with me. It's okay, though, at least I don't feel like I'm suffocating anymore.

By the time I make it down the steps, I see crowds of people pooling into groups while others head toward buses and parking lots. I'm suddenly glad for the clear fall day and the time it will take to walk home. Our apartment is less than a half-mile away with an extra bonus of Mom being at work. At least that's what her schedule said when I saw it stuck under the Marlboro magnet on the fridge.

I make it past the student parking lot and allow myself to relax for the first time since I woke up. Constantly being on guard is a daily exhaustion and it feels good to let go. I'll probably die from stomach ulcers by the time I'm forty but I figure that still gives me twenty-two good years.

Today didn't suck as much as I expected and I owe a lot of it to Brad. I almost hate to admit he was the best part of it, even though I had to fall on my ass to meet him. Humiliation almost stopped me from allowing his help, to say nothing of my usual steel barriers raised to keep out anyone I might possibly make a connection with. The strange thing was, it felt like he already knew me. He knew just how to put me at ease, even making me laugh when I was being ridiculously stubborn.

I can't deny Brad's attractive—girls definitely seem to notice him. One in particular gave me the stink eye when she saw us walking together. I wanted to laugh in her face because for once, I wasn't the outsider. But I didn't. I know how it feels to be on the other side. She shouldn't worry, I'll be keeping my focus on school and as soon as I graduate, I'm out of here.

I only need a few more credits to get my diploma and thankfully I have a total blow off schedule. I'm pretty sure the counselor thinks I've lost my mind, opting for two study halls instead of using senior privilege to go home early. But I know being at school—hell, anywhere but home—will help me focus. Besides, I never liked bringing schoolwork home when I could just do it there. No one will ever accuse me of being a procrastinator because like numbers I'm weird about homework, too. If I have an assignment, I just knock it out as soon as possible. I don't like things hanging over my head. Schoolwork is one thing I *can* control in my chaotic world.

If it weren't for my desire to go to college, I probably would've bailed on Mom already. But I need her, even if she is a complete mess. There's no way I can get an apartment on my own and also support myself. So I'll follow her rules until May. I don't have a choice, no matter where we end up.

I promised myself a while back that I would bust my ass and keep up my grade point average. I just hope it's enough to get some kind of academic scholarship. I know I won't go to Princeton or anything, but any state college will do. And whichever one puts the most miles between my mother and I will be the one I choose.

I'm a few blocks away from the school, looking up at the enormous pine trees, when I hear what sounds like a voice or maybe my name—I can't be sure. But I definitely heard something. I stop and scan the area, searching for someone who might have called for me, trying to figure out who would even know me. But there's no one around.

The house I'm stopped in front of looks like it's straight out of a Bates Motel movie. I saw it for the first time when Mom and I drove by a week ago. Even though it's old and abandoned it feels overwhelmingly inviting. Like I want to curl up on an imaginary porch swing and gaze at the sky. But there's something about it that makes me uneasy. Somehow it feels familiar, which is crazy since I've never even been to this town before, never mind anywhere near this house.

I'm almost sad to see the original white paint peeling away and all the windows boarded up. The house must have been amazing at one time and wonder why it's the only one on the street that's been left to rot. I scan over the house again, totally fascinated by it. The massive columns on the front porch frame the solid eight-panel double doors while its thick wood molding is covered with overgrown ivy, climbing up to the second story window.

The lawn is blanketed in tall grass and gigantic pine trees. A nightmare for any caretaker, if there were one. From where I'm standing, it looks like there's one window on the far left side that's not boarded up. I have to navigate a path to get a little closer and as I approach the window, I see that the glass has been completely broken out. Anyone or anything could easily sneak in with no problem. Which is a scary thought. What's even scarier is my overwhelming urge to go inside. And that's probably a really bad idea. There could be raccoons, or worse, hanging bats waiting to attack me.

Nope. I don't even want to mess with that. The thought of anything in there other than a cuddly dog or maybe a cat scares the crap out of me. Letting my instincts be my guide, I quickly turn around, telling myself to leave this place alone.

The path I took to get here is riddled with pinecones and I'm pretty sure they're the biggest ones I've ever seen. They're gorgeous, so perfectly symmetrical, and I pick one up just before stepping back on the sidewalk. The wind suddenly begins to pick up, whipping my hair around my face. I think I hear whispering, or maybe it's my name again?

What the hell?

I wait for a few more seconds, trying to talk myself out of doing something stupid. But curiosity is making it almost impossible to listen to my better judgment. I can't leave. I need to get inside that house. This time the urge is stronger. Instead of questioning it, I decide to just go for it, promising myself to be extra careful.

The second time I get to the window there's a cool breeze blowing on my face, but it's not coming from outside. It's coming from inside the house.

Very strange.

Maybe there's another open window I can't see yet?

Taking in a deep breath, I close my eyes, trying to prepare myself for anything. There could be decaying bodies, or animal carcasses, or something that's going to jump out at me. I'm not sure I'm ready, but force myself to slowly stretch my neck past the pane. It takes a couple of seconds for my eyes to adjust to the darkness, but then the room begins to lighten up. My eyes shift around what looks like a bedroom. It seems to have all of its original molding and wood floors. It's actually really pretty. Well, other than the stained mattress and scattered beer bottles all over the floor. Locals must use this as some sort of party spot.

Gross, but thankfully, no murder scenes or visible animals waiting to attack me. I probably shouldn't want to see more because tiny goosebumps are popping up and down my arms, but the need to keep going is starting to overwhelm me. Trying to stall for a few more seconds, I stand back and look up. The window, which is almost as tall as me, has leftover pieces of glass piling round the edges. Walking through will be the easy part. Once I'm in, there's no telling what or who could be inside.

Breathe, Candice.

Before I go any further, I stand quietly for a moment, listening. For a voice, for movement. Any sound. Anything that might make me change my mind away from the stupidity of sneaking into an old house. But it's no use. No matter how hard my gut pulls at me to walk away, I want to go in more. So I start making deals with myself.

Just take a few minutes. There's nothing waiting for you at home.

That was easy.

Taking another deep breath, I cautiously tiptoe over the threshold. There's a strong, musty odor, like an antique shop only five times worse. There's no telling how many leaks the roof has or how much rain has made it inside the window.

It's obvious this place is old, probably a hundred years or more. And there are so many doors going to God knows where that I'm back to questioning why I was crazy enough to come inside. I don't get a good feeling, and I'm about to talk myself into leaving when I sense something familiar. It's actually very comforting, but as quickly as it came it's gone again. Just like that.

That was weird.

Shrugging it off, I push the thought out of my head and keep going. I admire the fireplace molding, running my fingers along the dark wood tones and bronze inlay when suddenly, a sense of warmth touches my face. I turn in the direction it came from, quickly realizing it's only the sun's rays breaking through a cracked piece of wood above the broken window. But it's more than that. It's beyond soothing, as if the stress from the past twenty-four hours is being sucked out of my body. It feels amazing.

Bending my knees, I sit where I am, careful not to break the sun's connection or whatever this is because I don't want this incredible sensation to end. It's as if I'm in a warm bubble bath and having my back scratched at the same time; it's pure heaven.

I sit with my back against the wall for a while, adjusting myself to stay in the light as I watch the sun move across the room. I'm so relaxed I have to fight to keep my eyes open; I can feel myself drifting in and out. It doesn't take long for my lids feel like lead so I give in, feeling completely tranquil until my mind begins replaying the events from this morning with Mom. I can even smell the cigarettes and booze on her breath. I'm bracing myself for another smack when the scene suddenly changes and I see my father pushing me on a park swing. I'm maybe only five years old and I'm laughing as I beg him to push me harder. When he does, I instantly fall off, his voice screaming my name, becoming its own echo. I look up and can't see my dad anywhere because a black mist forms from the ground up, blacking out my vision. It's so dark that panic starts rising in my stomach because I know I'm alone. I hear my name and watch as the mist slowly begins to morph into the shape of a man.

My body starts to tremble and when I try to get up to run I'm frozen and can't do anything but watch. The black shadow man gets closer and reaches out, almost touching me. I open my mouth to scream but nothing comes out. He backs away immediately and I'm suddenly flushed with a renewed sense of calm. I'm no longer terrified, but just like the house, I sense something very alluring about him. When the shadow man reaches for me again, I flinch, jerking myself away. Everything fades.

My eyes pop open to an almost pitch black room. I'm disoriented but I can see dim light coming in through

the open window. Reality slams into my brain and I
bolt up.

I'm still in the house.

Holy shit!

My body doesn't have time to catch up with my
mind as I run as fast as I can, nearly tripping when I
jump through the window. I can feel the adrenaline
coursing through every single vein, my heart hammering against my chest. I can't get a deep breath and have
to stop. I'm so lightheaded I bend over, trying to get a
grip before I throw up.

I'm panicking and briefly pinch the inside of my
wrist, hoping it will take my mind off the nausea.

I don't want to throw up.

Please don't throw up.

I feel my watch instead and look down at the time. I
swallow the bile already in my throat because I can tell
it's late. My eyes go wide while my hand automatically
jerks to my mouth.

12:17?

In the morning?

Holy shit, how did I lose nearly nine hours?

CHAPTER SIX

ROM THE MOMENT she looked up at the house, I recognized her. I remained hidden and watched her approach the window, coaxing her to keep going. She was hesitant at first and even attempted to leave, but I brought her back, admiring her delicate features as she slid through the open frame. Her beauty took my breath away and it was everything I could do not to reach out and touch her long, honey strands as they dropped off her shoulder.

She drifted around the room, gliding her fingers across the mantle as if reminiscing about another time from years gone by. I hoped so badly she would recognize this house. I yearned to be the one she was touching. Decades have come and gone since I have felt her caress and I wanted more with each second we spent together.

So I made her stay.

My hands were within inches of her face. I could feel the warmth radiating from her beautiful skin. Almost instantly her eyes closed as I cradled her to the floor. Her soft flesh awoke a hunger in me—the kind of hunger a man feels for a woman. Her beauty was intoxicating and I came so close to kissing her enchanting lips, but I forced myself to pull back. I could not risk it; I must gain her trust first.

I held her close to me, savoring the feel of her body close to mine when without warning, troubling images slammed into my head. I could see what she saw and feel what she felt.

An overflowing river of sadness and anger crashed all around us and I understood—her world is dark. As I glimpsed into her past it made my connection with her even stronger. When I searched even deeper, I discovered that it is her own mother who is the burden of her torment. Intimidating and belittling her with words and actions, taking away the essence of the joyful girl she once was.

My rage became an entity of its own while I watched her dreadful memories play over and over.

I must help her.

I must protect her.

And I will, very soon.

CHAPTER SEVEN
~~CANDICE~~

I RACE BACK TO the apartment, hoping—no, praying—my mother isn't home. Or at the very least, passed out from a night of drinking. But no such luck. The kitchen light is on and I can see her through the window, sitting at the table with a drink in one hand and a cigarette in the other. My stomach drops. I'm in for it now.

I want to turn around and run but I know I'll have to face her eventually. I slowly open the door and calmly walk over to the table, scooting back a chair as I sit across from her. Hopefully there will be enough space for me to avoid a slap—or worse.

She doesn't say a word, she simply stares at me, cocking her head to the side as if in serious contemplation on how to murder me.

I'll try my best not to set her off; I don't want to say anything she could use against me. She's already fond of that little trick, but I have to come up with something. Anything to break the solid block of ice hanging between us. She reaches for her whiskey glass, pulling her eyes away from me, and downs the remaining sip.

I take it as my cue.

"I'm sorry...I fell asleep at a friend's house after school," I lie, but not entirely.

I watch little wrinkles form in the corner of her eyes as she peers back at me.

And there it is.

If she had the power to kill me with one look, I'd be a bloody mess on the floor.

Her fist pounds on the table. "Bullshit!"

I flinch but don't have time to react because she grabs the side of the table and jerks it up. The whiskey bottle slides down, spilling all over the floor, and when she suddenly lets go, the table slams back down, narrowly missing my foot. I'm startled by the crash and jolt out of my chair, crouching as I back away from her like some kind of frightened animal. Mom means business and I dread what will come next. She's beyond fast, a whiskey-fueled leopard, and I am once again her prey. Before I know it, her hand cracks across my face. It burns instantly. I have no doubt there's a trail of red welts on my cheek.

"You lie to me again and you won't be able to talk at all! Tell me the truth!" Her breath reeks as usual and I try like hell not to let it show on my face.

"It's the truth, Mom! I really did fall asleep," I say, trying to ignore the hard sting on my cheek.

She stares at me for a minute as I secretly pray for the old Mom to come out and laugh, saying she was only kidding. She always did have a sick sense of humor.

"Your curfew is midnight, Goddammit! And not a second after!" She staggers and points her finger at me like it somehow increases the severity of her words. "This isn't over, little missy. Not by a long shot!"

She backs away and blinks as if tired of dealing with me, fumbling to reach another half empty whiskey bottle from the counter. Not a normal reaction, but I'm suddenly grateful for the late hour and the alcohol that might have made her world spin.

I watch her stumble away in a drunken haze, hoping like hell she won't remember this in the morning.

~~

It takes exactly thirteen steps to walk from one side of my room to the other. I feel like a caged animal, waiting for someone to open the trapdoor so I can bolt and never look back. I'm fully aware that I may not sleep tonight, trying to piece together what happened in that house. I assume it's what a caffeine overdose feels like when the anxiety sets in. Only time will fix it. But there has to be some kind of reasonable explanation why I basically passed out for almost nine hours. It scares me that I have an intense yearning to go back. Maybe I'm having some kind of psychotic or bipolar breakdown? The only thing missing is a straightjacket and a thread of drool hanging from my mouth.

It's quite possible this last move has finally broken me. I'm already living the life of a gypsy because no matter where we end up, no place ever feels like home. It's borderline torture living with a mother who doesn't remotely act like one. Lately, everything sets her off and her red-hot temper is getting worse. The constant abuse she puts her body through can't be helping, either.

Sometimes I think I'm a bad person for hating her, but the truth is, I actually don't hate her at all. I hate what she's become. She contradicts everything a mother should be and now she's merely surviving. Mom's never been a nurturer and she has no mercy for weakness, but as strange as it sounds, those two things have become her strengths. I just hope she uses them when she finds her next guy. But that might be wishful thinking. It's true what they say about old dogs and new tricks.

I have less than five hours before school starts. I wasn't planning on staying up all night, but I don't think I have a choice. Before I lose my mind, I need to occupy my brain and try to relax while I still have some time. Besides, I have all day tomorrow to be freaked out.

Thankfully, I have a stack of Jane Austen books on my dresser. I reach for *Pride and Prejudice* because it's my favorite. I've read it at least ten times and it never fails to take me to another place. And, no matter where I begin, Mr. Darcy and Elizabeth Bennet eventually end up together and live happily ever after.

I'm about to climb in bed when I realize I'm still in the clothes I wore to school, so I undress and put on my favorite oversized t-shirt. I almost forgot how much comfort this old thing gives me. Especially now. It belonged to my father and was one of the few things he left behind. I've treasured it all this time and have probably given it more sentimental value than it's worth. I thought for sure my dad would want it back and the first year after he left, I held out hope that he would. At the time, I didn't realize it was me he should have come back for, not some random piece of clothing. Eventually, that fantasy was replaced with reality. He's never coming back. All I have is this dumb t-shirt. It's riddled with holes from too many washings but that doesn't matter. It knows all my secrets and holds so many tears and as silly as it sounds, it somehow represents home, even when it never feels like I have one.

~~

The alarm goes off and I wake up in the same position I was in when I got into bed. I don't remember falling asleep or dreaming at all. My book is open on my chest, but it's like I woke up from a black hole of nothing.

Shrugging it off, I pull my body of out bed and make my way to the mirror. The first thing I notice is Mom's handprint on my face. It's not nearly as red as it was last night, but it's still slightly warm to the touch and definitely noticeable. Fortunately, I've become a master at applying concealer and I can make almost any mark disappear. Hopefully no one will notice. But, to be safe, I should definitely wear my hair down.

Swiping a dab of foundation on my cheek, I blend it in, trying not to press too hard. The bruise is deep and will take a while to go away. Mom still has a wicked right hook, even dead drunk.

I shake away the growing pity party. It's a waste of time to feel sorry for myself. I'm like Mom in that way because after she divorced Dad, it toughened her up. She never dwelled on the fact that he cheated on her and couldn't support us. She simply moved on and didn't talk about him. She can totally turn it off when she needs to and I admire that about her. I'm the only one who sees the internal wounds left behind.

I'm pretty sure a few of Mom's biggest scars came from a guy named Russ. She met him right after the divorce so technically he was the rebound guy. Mom had been waiting tables at a local dive while we were living in East Texas and unfortunately, he moved in with us after only after a couple of weeks. Even at thirteen, I could tell he was an abusive alcoholic. But all Mom wanted to do was make him happy, so she started drinking with him. It worked for a while because he had a drinking buddy and free rent. I'm pretty sure he knew I saw through him, so he steered clear of me. When he became verbally and physically abusive towards her, it was as if Mom lost all self-worth. She was suddenly an insecure teenager who only liked the guy who treated her like shit.

Several times it got so bad Mom had to call the police, and if she didn't, the neighbors would. Russ ended up spending a night or two in jail but Mom would always take him back, never pressing charges to keep him away for good.

After his fifth arrest for assault, the cop at our door pulled Mom aside. I'll never forget watching his face change when he saw me sitting in the corner with my legs to my chest. A look of disgust washed over his features and then he turned back to Mom and said, "Lady, if you keep putting up with this, then you're the sick one." The blank stare on her face made me think he was just talking to deaf ears but for some reason—or miracle, I'm not quite sure—Mom finally listened to that cop. Thank goodness. I might've been next.

From that point on, I knew Mom kept her demons close, but now her tough, independent nature has been replaced with anger and doing almost anything, like finding drinking buddies at work or taking extra shifts, not to feel alone. Even keeping me around. She clearly doesn't want me anymore but I guess someone is better than no one.

I take one more look at myself in the mirror before heading out, satisfied with how well I've concealed the mark of drunken fury. Thankfully she's still in her room, but I know she's awake. Smoke is beginning to cloud up the entire house even though her door is closed. I don't dare disturb her so I shut the front door as quietly as humanly possible. I almost don't need an alarm clock when I've got a smoke reeking up the place. She's one step away from setting off the smoke detector.

The second I step outside the humidity hits me like a brick wall and I wonder why I even bothered doing my hair. It's September, how the hell can it be this cool yet be so freaking humid at the same time?

Frustrated, I gather it to one side, accidently touching the bruise on my cheek and catching whiff of my sleeve. The cigarette smell isn't as strong as the apartment, but it's still there. Reaching into my backpack, I duck behind a parked car and look both ways. No one's around so I pull out a small bottle of watered down peach body spray I keep with me when I can find it on sale at the store. Taking one more look both ways I douse myself, practically using half of the bottle before slipping it back in a side pocket.

At least today I won't smell like an ashtray.

~~

I'm about a block away from the house, the strange and amazing place where I lost hours of my life, my mind on overdrive as I try to think of every possible scenario that could explain how I blacked out. My thoughts are interrupted by blaring music from behind me. Glancing over my shoulder, I see a silver Porsche passing to my right. I turn and lock eyes with Brad Davis. The Porsche suddenly screeches to a halt and backs up next to me.

I stop where I am and watch his lips curl up as his window slides down. He's about to say something when a truck comes within inches of slamming into him. Brad looks in his rearview mirror, waving as the truck swerves around and honks, leaving a trail of smoky skid marks. Laughter and a middle finger shoot out from the driver's side as Brad shoots one back, grinning the entire time.

Apparently they know each other.

Without skipping a beat, his eyes are back on me. "Hey, you. Need a ride?" he asks, raising one eyebrow.

He's cute as hell.

I try to hold back my reaction, because God help me, he looks exceptionally good this morning. My mind is racing on what to do next. I turn my head and contemplate for a second, remembering the house of euphoria literally steps away. I left the apartment early so I could look around a little more, maybe check if there's some kind of gas leak. But when I glance back again, his sexy brown eyes and two-day-old stubble make him hard to resist. I like what I see and hate myself for it.

"Yeah, sure." I smile back, cursing myself for bending my own rules. I'm not here to make friends—or anything else.

Brad immediately jumps out of the car, following me over to the passenger side. He waits until I'm close then opens my door and I slip in. When I look up, he's leaning forward, smiling down at me.

"You look really nice."

"Yeah?" I smile and roll my eyes. "I'm sure you say that to all the girls."

"Nope, just the pretty ones." He winks and shuts the door.

I fasten my seatbelt, my eyes following his stride as he walks over to his side. He seems to have the confidence of a way older guy and his gray t-shirt and tight Levi's accentuate how good he must look underneath. I can tell he's got some hair on his chest, too. Most girls don't like that, but I'm a sucker for it.

Damn him.

He opens his door and glides in like a professional NASCAR driver, starting the engine with an efficient flick of the wrist. I try to hide the fact that I'm checking out his hands, his arms, his neck, even his lips. Everything about him is making me question why I made those stupid *no boyfriend* rules. I can't deny he's got my attention.

"I could have walked the four extra blocks," I say, trying to act nonchalant as I place my backpack on the floorboard.

His hand pushes the stick shift into first gear and he looks me square in the eyes. "Not if I'm around."

Suddenly I'm a ball of nerves and realize I probably like him more than I want to admit. But I'm also beating myself up for it. I know it's not a good idea to date and it never will be as long as my home life is a mess. I try not to let the tension show on my face even though my heart is racing.

Brad makes a left into the "seniors only" parking before shutting off the engine. He looks down, as if contemplating something, then looks over at me.

"We've got a little time. Wanna talk?"

I nod and try not to blurt out something stupid. The first time I met him, my anxiety was on high alert...or maybe I was too preoccupied to notice he was anything more than just a cute guy. But now, with him sitting so close, looking at me with those ridiculous brown eyes, I'm starting to feel uncomfortable. So I do what any apprehensive, eighteen-year-old girl sitting in a car next a hot guy would do. Absolutely nothing. I just sit, waiting for him to start talking, hoping the awkward moment will pass.

"So, where do you live?" he asks, dropping his gaze down to my lips.

"We." I pause, trying to ignore the fact that he's looking at my mouth. "My mom and I just moved here. We haven't found a house yet, so we're staying at the Nantucket apartments."

Which is my standard answer, the "looking for a house" part. It feels less pathetic than admitting we'll probably never live in a house again. I hadn't noticed until now that I look at my hands when I lie. I glance back up and he's still smiling. Maybe he bought it?

Brad reaches for the radio, turning up the volume, and the awkwardness melts away with the music.

Maybe he could feel it too?

I instantly close my eyes, mentally singing every word to an Erasure song. Nobody knows I love to sing. Not even Mom. At my last school, I tried out for the concert choir and made it. But Mom had different plans and yanked me out of that school, too. It sucked because the music director said I showed a lot of potential. Apparently I have perfect pitch. He even said I could probably work up to doing solos. For once, I was excited about going to a new school, but when we moved here, I didn't even ask Mrs. Stephens if they had a choir. I couldn't risk having to leave something I loved so much again. So I only signed up for the exact courses I needed to graduate and nothing more.

I open my eyes, slightly embarrassed that I got lost in the song for a moment and look over at Brad. He's smiling and looking right at me.

"You're a great singer."

"I was humming. How'd you hear me over the music?"

"I'm a good listener." He grins and I shake my head, smiling back at him.

And just like that, I'm right back to being uncomfortable. It doesn't help that I've only dated a couple of guys and neither of them amounted to more than a few dates and a kiss here or there. I don't get that kind of inexperienced vibe from Brad. He's definitely way more confident than me and I can tell he's had his fair share of girlfriends.

A distant bell rings and I immediately reach for the door handle when Brad touches my arm.

"It's only the first bell. We have some time."

"Okay," I say, trying to refocus. I don't know what to say next, but figure I should talk about something harmless.

"I like your car." I glance over to him and smile, rubbing the leather seat with my fingers.

"Thanks. It was my dad's. He was about to trade it in but I begged him to give it to me instead. My mom thought it was a bad idea though." He smiles as if reliving the moment.

"Is it your first car?"

"No, I had an old beat up Nova that was on its last leg. So really, I needed something right away."

"Well, that was lucky," I say, glancing back up at him when he turns to face me.

"Yeah, that's what my mom keeps telling me."

"I hope it's not running out. You were practically rear-ended by a truck just now."

He laughs. "That was Nick. He's a good guy, but kind of an asshole." He touches my hand, and I look up to his smile. "Besides, my chivalry is without limits."

Laughing louder than I should, I look over at his now serious face, swallowing the golf ball-sized lump in my throat.

"Oh, God, you were serious?" I manage.

He leans in closer, only inches from my face as he gently squeezes my fingers. Even though I'm not looking up at him, his gaze practically devours me. My stomach tightens as if a thousand butterflies are at war.

Yeah, he's light years ahead of me with experience.

"If you ever need a ride, just call me," he says, letting go of my hand as he opens the glove box and takes out a pen. His arm then reaches behind the seat, pulling a notebook from his backpack. He rips off a corner of paper, quickly writes something down, and hands it to me.

"And yes, I am serious. Here's my number."

"Thanks." I glance down, folding it twice before shoving it in my pocket. "But I really do like to walk."

Lord, even his handwriting is sexy.

This is not what I'd planned. It feels like my world is starting to spin out of control because just sitting here next to him is making me doubt every rule I set for myself before we got here. I've only known him for two days and I already know he deserves better than this, better than me. He could have any girl in school—he doesn't need some loser with a crazy mother who'll probably be gone by Christmas. Just thinking about moving again makes me want to cry.

I turn slightly in my seat, facing away from him, and close my eyes, hoping he doesn't think I'm some kind of head case.

Shit.

Shit.

Shit.

"I hope you're not just feeling sorry for me," I blurt out without thinking. I can't look at him because I can feel him staring at me.

"Is that what you think?" He pauses for a second then says, "You want the truth?"

I look straight at him because in my world, honesty is rare.

"You fascinate me," he admits, still keeping his eyes focused on me.

"Oh" is all I manage to say as I continue looking out the window. *What the hell does that mean?*

He goes on, his voice softening. "And before you think too much about it, it's a good thing." He squeezes my hand again. "Okay?"

I turn to look at him again and his brows raise. He's waiting for me to say something.

"Okay," I answer, watching his face light up into a smile.

After a few seconds, he interrupts the clumsy silence. "C'mon, I'll walk you to first period."

There is a God.

He gets out of the car and I linger a few more seconds, hoping he doesn't notice that I'm studying him from the corner of my eye. He makes me nervous, but in a good way. I have no idea what I'm going to do with him so I suck in a breath and let it out just before he opens my door. He leans in with another sexy grin.

"I mean it, Candice. You can call me anytime. And not just for rides."

CHAPTER EIGHT

~~**BRAD**~~

I PRACTICALLY GAVE MYSELF whiplash when her blond hair caught my eye on the way to school this morning. I knew it was Candice before she even looked at me. She seemed preoccupied and I hated the look on her face when she asked if I was giving her a ride out of pity. I couldn't help noticing there was something behind those blue eyes that was troubling her. Just thinking about it pulls at my gut. I had to set things right and let her know that was the last thing I thought. Hopefully I didn't push it too far. It's hard to hold back with a girl like her. I wanted to kiss her so badly but I could tell she's not ready for that. The intensity of the feelings I have for her are beyond crazy. It's like I'm under some kind of spell.

I thought I needed a break from girls all together after Sarah and I split up. I couldn't stand her neediness and bullshit drama. I knew right away she was trouble and I let her play mind games for way too long. I'm not proud that the only thing we had going for us was chemistry; that only goes so far.

My first impression of Candice wasn't great. I figured when she didn't want my help getting up she was just stuck up, like all the other girls in this school. I had sworn off dating anyway, so why would I care? But after spending just a few minutes with her it was obvious that she was the complete opposite of every girl I've dated. Sure, she's new, but it's more than that. It's her vulnerability and the way she kept pushing me away that I wasn't expecting. All I know is meeting her has changed my mind on more than just dating again. I'm pretty sure she's got some solid walls built up but I want to know everything about her life. Where she's from, what she likes to do, and most of all, if she'll consider a guy like me.

Chapter Nine

~~Candice~~

I'M ABOUT TO walk into my third period class when I feel a tap on my shoulder. Turning around, I see my counselor, Mrs. Stephens, staring at me with a concern in her eyes.

"Hi, Candice. Are you finding all your classes?"

"Oh, yes, thanks."

"Great!" she says with a troubled look on her face. I'm not sure that's what she really wanted to ask.

What's going on with her?

"That's good. I just…" She stops, dropping her eyes to my cheek, then back to me.

Shit.

She takes me by the arm, leading me toward the ladies' room like we're about to have a secret meeting, stopping once we're inside. "Is everything all right, honey?" she whispers with a new look of concern.

My hand goes directly to my bruised cheek as if covering it up will make her forget what she saw. "Uh huh…

everything's fine," I lie, watching her face contort, because I'm sure she knows I'm lying.

As if dismissing my words, she says, "You know I'm here to help, right?"

I nod, not meeting her eyes.

"Good, because I mean it, Candice. If you need to talk about anything, all you have to do is knock on my door."

"Okay, thank you." I smile as genuinely as I can before walking out into the hallway.

"Oh, and Candice?"

"Yeah?" I look back at her.

"Do you have a car?"

Where did that come from?

"No, but I live pretty close. Why?"

She looks both ways as if she's afraid someone might be listening. "Just be careful walking home."

"Um, yeah. Sure," I answer, no doubt with a confused look on my face. Because I am. Are there boogeymen on the streets in this town or something?

She takes my hand and I immediately see the worry in her eyes. "Just promise me." She closes her mouth and swallows once. "Please."

The bell rings and I nod, knowing I have to haul my butt to class or be late. I pull my hand out of her grip, walking so fast I may as well be running.

I hate being late and despise having an entire class stare at me when I am. It's happened enough times you'd think I'd be used it. But the panic that slams into my chest when a room full of strangers suddenly focuses all their attention on me is different each and every time. And just like that, I start resenting being the new girl—and my mother—all over again.

Thank goodness I don't have to go to my locker because it's a miracle I make it to class just in the nick of time. Unfortunately, my seat is next to a guy who talks to himself and likes to shoot spit wads.

Awesome.

On the positive side, World History is one of my favorite classes and we just started a chapter on the European Renaissance. As much as I love this era, I keep going back to the conversation I just had with Mrs. Stephens. I hope like hell she doesn't try to call Mom, or worse, Child Protective Services. I could tell by the look on her face that she saw the mark on my cheek. It's like she knew where to look. But how?

After torturing myself with question after question, I decide I just can't obsess about it and should probably pay attention. The teacher, a leggy bleached blond who looks too old for her bright skirt and high heels, is writing something on the board. I notice only one guy is paying attention, the rest are checking out her ass.

Typical.

Mentally rolling my eyes, I pull out my spiral notebook, watching the girl next to me raise her hand when the teacher asks if anyone knows how many wives King Henry VIII executed. That's a no-brainer for me and if this is any indication of how this class will be all semester, I could probably test out right now.

"Yes, you in the back," the teacher says, pointing in her direction.

"Two," she answers as a spit wad soars past my face.

I don't think the teacher saw it, but Jesus, who the hell does that? I shoot Talks-to-Himself a dirty look and he immediately slides down in his seat. Good. Maybe I embarrassed him. I'm pretty sure he's not in the popular group and I'm instantly ashamed of the smile I'm trying to hide. Fortunately, it worked, but he's sitting with his head down on the desk. I'm not sure if I hurt his feelings or he's simply taking a nap.

I manage to finish what was supposed to be a homework assignment in class. I know everything there is to know about Henry VIII, and don't even have to crack open the book to answer the two-page worksheet. It also kept my mind occupied for a beautiful ten minutes.

I shove my pen and notebook in my backpack when the bell rings, feeling around in the bottom for the quarters I threw in a couple days ago. For the first time in days, I'm starving and lunch sounds good for a change.

~~~

The double doors to the cafeteria are almost completely blocked. I can't believe how many people are already in lines and sitting at tables. I'll likely have a panic attack before I get a chance to eat anything. Making matters worse, the noise in here is ear piercing. Amazingly, I'm able to make my way to the vending machines in the back without being elbowed in the ribs and spot an empty table in a corner.

Placing my Diet Coke and Snickers on a napkin, I'm about to take a bite when I'm tapped on the shoulder. I'm a little startled but manage not to jump as I look up and see Brad grinning down at me.

"You don't have to sit alone." He tilts his head, gesturing to the table across from mine. He must pick up on my uncomfortable vibe and says, "C'mon, I'll protect you," and winks, taking my hand like he does it every day.

So of course, I cave.

Again.

The table is full of jocks in letter jackets and uniformed cheerleaders and for a split-second, I feel like I've walked onto the movie set of *Heathers*. I curse myself for letting Brad take me away from a table where no one noticed me. I'm not ready to chat with a bunch of strangers, and it doesn't help when everyone stops talking and stares at us when Brad pulls out my chair.

He waves his hand and says, "M'lady" like some kind of medieval prince as I place my sorry excuse for a lunch on the table. Even though it's impossibly loud in here, a few of the guys must have been entertained by what Brad did or said because they laugh.

Brad places his hand in the small of my back. "Everyone, this is Candice." Then he looks down at me, waving his hand like he's a butler at the Vanderbilt mansion. "Candice, this is everyone."

Laughter, nods, and even a few "heys" are immediately directed our way, welcoming me to their exclusive lunch club. The only thing I can do is smile like I mean it, so I do, and within seconds, their attention is onto something else.

Thank God.

Taking a deep breath of relief, I bite off the top quarter of my candy bar. I almost can't believe how amazing it tastes. I'm pretty sure I even moaned a little but it's so loud in here, I can't tell.

"That's all you're eating?" Brad's brows push together as he pulls up next to me, visibly troubled by my poor nutritional choices.

"I'm—I'm not that hungry," I lie, taking a sip from my Coke.

His eyes drop down to my mouth and if I didn't know better, I'd swear he can tell I'm a little turned on by it when he smiles, shaking his head.

"You know, around seventh period that sugar high is gonna make you crash and burn."

I cock my head, wondering why he's so concerned about what I'm eating after seeing his lunch.

"And you think that huge slice of dripping grease is a better choice?" Immediately, I want to punch my own face for flirting with him.

"Hey, I'm eating protein and carbs, like a good boy," he explains, sporting his signature cocky grin. "Tomatoes are even a vegetable. Or a fruit or something."

Now he's flirting back. Hell, I don't think he ever stopped. I contemplate ways to save myself from this conversation until he interrupts.

"Got any plans tomorrow night?" he asks, taking another bite of the drooping slice of pizza.

"Uh, I don't know, why?" I also don't know why I'm engaging in this making plans thing.

"A few of us are going to the movies. You wanna come?" His perfect smile reveals his perfect teeth and I want to bang my head against the wall.

I don't know what to say because I can't date him. I can't date anyone. Complications in my life makes it not an option so before this goes any further, I have to tell him. He's been so nice to me and deserves that much, but the room is somehow getting louder and everyone is staring at me again.

Keeping my sanity is the only thing I have left. I have to get out of here before the panic sets in and I'm a complete, embarrassed mess. So I stand up and clean my spot even though there isn't anything to clean.

"Sorry, I gotta go," I say to Brad, practically sprinting out of the cafeteria.

Impossibly over the deafening chatter in the room, I actually hear what sounds like a chair scooting across the floor.

"Candice, wait!" Brad's voice hits me like a knife.

Shit.

Seconds later, he catches up to me, gently gripping the top of my arm. I turn around to find him looking at me like I'm insane.

"What did I say?" he asks, already apologizing with his eyes.

I shrug, trying like hell to look calm. This is too much. He is too much, so I blurt the first thing I can think of. "Why are you so interested in me?"

He looks at me like he didn't hear me right, so I repeat the question.

"Why are you so..." I take a deep breath because he's staring at me in the middle of the cafeteria. "So interested in me?"

His eyebrows go up. "I—I just am." The look on his face tells me two things. He's being sincere, and without a doubt, I like him way more than I realized until this moment. But I'm not the girl for him. He should be with one of those giggly cheerleaders eyeballing me at the table. Not someone like me who can barely walk into a crowded room without getting hives. I'm constantly straddling a thin line between chaos and insanity and he deserves better.

I look up and see hope in his brown eyes and can hardly get the words out. This is going to be harder than I thought. "You've been so nice..."

"Wait," he interrupts and looks around the room like he's about to say something he only wants me to hear. "Just come as my friend. That's all I want."

My heart is beating so fast and I'm silently cursing the tears welling up and betraying me at the worst possible moment.

Brad notices right away and takes my hand. "Come with me."

So I do.

He leads me around the hordes of people, cutting through lines of students still waiting for their food, finally stopping just outside the cafeteria doors. "Tell me what I did and I'll fix it."

His eyes are intense and focused only on me. Even a guy who walks by, calling his name, is ignored. It's uncomfortable when he gives me all his attention and no one else. So, I decide to tell him the truth because I don't ever do that anymore. I've become the martyr of deceit. Clearly, Mom has taught me well.

"Nothing. You didn't do anything." I half turn and he pulls my arm back, clearing his throat. I don't have to look at his face to know he's confused by my actions. So I try to explain once more.

"You barely know me and I've been nothing but strange and well, standoffish. I'm just not used to this." Before I know it, my stupid tears begin to blur my vision.

"Used to what?" he asks, almost in a whisper. Like if he talks in a normal voice I'll shatter into bits right here.

I look up at his brown eyes, the concern on his face making me pissed at myself for getting so emotional.

"This kind of attention," I reply, blinking as a warm tear drops down my cheek.

His expression changes, like all of a sudden he gets what I've been going through. Almost as if he's seeing inside my soul for the first time and he pulls me into his chest. The first thing I notice is how good he smells. All I want to do is stand like this forever. I haven't been held in so long and when his hand cradles my head I can't believe I'm questioning anything about him.

"Listen," he says, still whispering like he's talking to a scared child, "I like you, and I think we could be friends. We could have fun together. But if you're uncomfortable with that, I won't ask again. If you really don't want to go, I mean. But I hope you'll change your mind."

His other arm is around my neck and I have to really look up because he's much taller than me, especially this close. His brown eyes are speckled with green and seem much too perfect to be real. I feel my stomach tighten at the thought of something more with him.

He leans down and kisses my forehead and my eyes close automatically.

"And if you're uncomfortable in a big group of people, we can deal with that. You don't seem to mind when it's just me and you."

He's right, being with him one on one doesn't bother me at all. In fact, I really like it. And when he holds me like this I like it even more.

I'm not sure if it's his sincerity or the fact that I'm too emotionally spent to argue, but I want to give him an answer. It's as if he's a raging river, and I'm swirling in the rapids. Maybe for once I should allow myself to let go and drift over to the other side.

"Okay," I say, looking back up at his face and hoping I don't regret this.

"Okay, what?" His brows push together.

"I'll go with you tomorrow."

His expression is worth the sacrificial lamb I just killed to say those words.

"And I want popcorn."

CHAPTER TEN

~~CANDICE~~

I'M ABOUT TO open my locker when I hear someone call my name. I know the voice and when I look up, I see Brad walking straight toward me. It's been two whole class periods since I last saw him and somehow he's managed to look even better than before. How is that possible?

"Hey, you," he says, already flashing me his signature grin.

"Hey." I smile back because I can't help it.

"Need a ride home?" he asks, looking at me with his incredible brown eyes.

I'm too mentally drained to check out the house anyway. After dealing with crowded hallways, my weird conversation with Mrs. Stephens, and at least one mini-panic attack, a ride home sounds pretty good. Besides, it gets dark earlier every night and the thought of looking around a mysterious house when it's pitch black makes me beyond nervous.

"Sure."

~~

We're several cars back, waiting our turn to exit the parking lot, when he reaches for my hand between shifting gears. Piece by piece, I can feel my walls starting to crumble. It seems effortless for him to show that he cares even though neither of us is talking. We don't have to. It's a strange yet amazing moment of companionship as we share space together and just be. I can take a deep breath and for the first time today, my stomach isn't tied up in knots..

Brad makes a right out of the parking lot, waving at the same dude in the truck who nearly rear ended him this morning.

"Is he that Nick guy?" I ask.

"Yeah. Good memory." He shifts into neutral because we've stopped again and then takes my hand. "He and his girlfriend are coming with us to the movies tomorrow."

"Okay. Glad I'm not riding with him." I laugh.

"Shit, I'm more afraid of his girlfriend. She's a trip." He shakes his head, shifting the stick into first.

"Really? Why?"

"For starters, she's up his ass constantly and she's jealous of every girl who comes within five feet of him," he says, shaking his head. "The chick wears me out."

"Wow, that's gotta suck."

"Yeah, it really does." He glances over at me and sighs. "She has to be home by midnight, though, so that's when we go off on our own. Otherwise, she'd be with us, too."

"We?"

"Oh, yeah. Me, Nick, and Paul," he answers, still holding my hand.

"Where do you go?" I ask, wondering where they could possibly go after midnight in this small town.

"Usually to the old Emory house. We can't always get beer, but Nick usually has pot." He laughs. "His parents don't know he's figured out where they keep their stash."

Where have I heard that name before?

"The Emory house?" I say, genuinely intrigued.

"Yeah, it's one of the old mansions on Oak Lawn." He pauses as if he's just thought of something. "You were right by it this morning. It's the one that's all boarded up, but you can get in if you walk around to the side."

My heart starts beating a little faster because I know exactly what house he's talking about and exactly how they got in.

Trying to sound oblivious, I ask another question I'm not sure I want the answer to. "So, no one lives there?"

"No, it's been like that for as long as I can remember," he replies.

I can't help myself and have to ask. "Do you know why?"

Brad's lips get tight and he drops my hand like a hot potato. "Kind of...I mean, you hear things over the years." He pauses and I see his jaw start to twitch. "I'm pretty sure the same family who built it still owns it." He briefly looks out the window and says, "Rumor has it, someone died there. I think that's why it was abandoned."

"Wow, how sad," I say, trying to keep my voice as calm as possible. "Do you know who died?"

"I think it was the son, Atticus."

I don't have time to think because he snaps me back into reality.

"Which turn is it? The first or second?"

"Oh, the first one," I answer, grabbing my backpack from the floorboard.

He pulls in and I point to the stairs that lead up to our door. He looks for a second as if making a mental note then asks, "What's your apartment number?"

"1316."

His lips curl up as if I've handed him a secret key, but he's clearly over what was bothering him before. He leans forward, bringing his lips only inches from my ear. "Pick you up tomorrow?"

I'm caught off guard when the intimacy of his gesture sends a sexual surge through my body. And I like it. "Okay," I say, a little out of breath as I reach for the handle.

"Wait." His hand is back on mine for a second before his door opens. He quickly hops out, jogging over to my side.

I can't pull my eyes off him and have to take a deep breath. I've never felt this kind of attraction toward any guy and again, want to bang my head against a wall.

"M'lady," he says again. Only this time he takes my hand and pulls me close. I can't help but smile because I'm torn between the need to run like hell and the desire for him—this—to become an everyday thing.

"Back to being a medieval prince?" I ask, trying to hide my sudden nervousness because old habits die hard and he just can't be for real. How did I not see it before? I'm not dealing with an ordinary guy.

I watched Brad awe everyone he talked to today. He's not just the Big Man on Campus, he appears to actually be a good person. He's funny, he's hot, and he's the kind of guy every other guy wants to be. And if he tries to kiss me right now, I'll probably melt into a puddle right here in the parking lot.

"Something like that." He leans down, lacing his fingers through mine as he gently kisses my cheek. I swear he's going to kill me with his slow movements; it gives me too much time to think about what he's doing. I look up at him and he waits a few seconds before opening his eyes.

Dear God.

"See ya tomorrow," he says, still holding my hand.

I'm biting my lip, trying to fill my lungs with air so I can respond. "Yes," I finally say, pulling my hand away from his as I turn to walk up the steps.

I glance over just before unlocking my front door and see that he's already back in his car, looking up at me. When our eyes catch he smiles and it's pretty clear he's waiting to make sure I'm safely inside before he leaves. I have to catch my breath. Nobody has cared enough about me to make sure I get into a building safely. He—this—scares the crap out of me. I have no idea where it's going. Hell, I'm not even sure this is a good idea, but spending time with him is starting to blur my own judgment. I smile and shoot him a quick wave and he nods as I pull the door behind me.

I'm in trouble.

The familiar stench of cigarette smoke yanks me back into reality. I can't stand it and jog over to the window, pulling the curtains aside as I push the frame all the way up. Instantly, a cool breeze flows in, hitting my face. I'm grateful for fresh air—part of me feels like I should sit right here until Mom gets home and complains that it's cold. I'm pretty sure she's never even considered cracking a window, let alone smoking outside. And I don't dare suggest it. Mom doesn't like being questioned; it might make her look bad. Even to herself.

I trip on a pair of jeans as I reach for my backpack. The room is a total pigsty. It's a miracle I made it all the way from the door to the window without falling all over myself. I don't remember it looking this bad this morning. When Mom is stressed, she thinks the living room is her closet and personal trashcan. It's amazing how quickly she can destroy a room and if I don't clean it up, it'll only get worse. So I begin picking up the random clothes, shoes, and newspapers—you name it, her crap is scattered everywhere.

I don't mind this new chore. Cleaning allows me to think but still feel like I'm accomplishing something at the same time. Already, my thoughts are racing from one subject to another. Brad pops in first. It feels like my heart can't understand why my mind keeps trying to push him away. I'm torn with what to do with him and I'm nervous all over again. Seconds later, my mind shifts to the old, mysterious house. A place where I lost hours of my life and I can't explain why. The *not knowing why* part intrigues yet terrifies the hell out of me and my stomach twists the new knots starting to form a little tighter. I need to go back to that house. I need to get to the bottom of what happened one way or another.

Stuffing the last of the cigarette butts and old newspapers in a used grocery bag, I heave a satisfied sigh. The room looks and smells a ton better. I close the window and fix the curtains because the wind is getting stronger. I take a moment to stare out, watching the trees sway in the breeze.

"Someone died there. I think it was the son."

Suddenly, I want to know everything because I still feel a strong, strange connection to it and I have no clue why. There has to be a logical explanation. It's been in the back of my mind all day, never leaving my thoughts entirely. The house made me feel welcome, like it knew what I needed at the precise moment, melting all my anxiety away. It's as if it has a conscience and that's impossible.

Tomorrow. Tomorrow I will go back and come hell or high water, I will have the answers.

~~

By the time Mom comes home, everything is spotless and dinner is ready. My attempt at softening her up has a fifty-fifty chance if she remembers our fight. The planets must have aligned or Jesus had some extra mercy to give because she's actually in a good mood for once.

To be safe, I better keep my guard up just in case.

The responsible party for Mom's temporary happiness is some guy named Tom who also happens to be a big tipper. Apparently, right after Mom started her new waitressing job he became one of her regulars and "totally digs" her first name. Especially the way she spells Daisee with a double E because "it's just about the cutest thing he's ever seen."

Barf.

I can't help my mental eye roll because I have no doubt he's just trying to get in her pants. It's almost comical that she can't see through his money and compliments. I hope by some miracle he ends up being a good guy because when Mom falls for someone, she falls hard. And if it goes south like it usually does, I become her target. With any luck, this new guy will keep her occupied, even if it's for a little while. All I need is enough time to investigate what the hell is going on with that house.

Mom sits down on the sofa, looking around as if suddenly noticing how clean the apartment is.

"Looks nice in here." She smiles at me for the first time in a while. It's about the closest thing she'll come to saying thank you, and that's okay. She hasn't learned she can no longer hurt me on the inside.

"I made some rice and beans," I say, walking back from the kitchen, handing her a full bowl with a spoon. I'll do anything tonight to keep the peace while she seems willing to be pleasant.

I sit across from her and watcher as she devours the food. "Glad your job is working out." I smile, hoping to get more information out of her. It's always good to know what your nemesis is up to.

She looks up at me with her mouth half full. "Yeah, it's going okay." She swallows before finishing her thought. "Tom thinks I should get a job somewhere else that pays more money." She gets up and walks to the kitchen, placing her bowl in the sink.

I'm immediately astonished.

"Are you going to start looking again?" I ask, hoping she's not already thinking of bailing on this place, too.

"Nah, I like it there." She lights a cigarette. "And the manager thinks I can take over his job with some training."

I didn't realize I was holding my breath until she finished. "Oh, is he leaving?"

"Maybe. He's not sure yet." She takes another puff. "His wife wants to move back to Dallas, where they're from."

Smoke billows out of her nose, making slow, swirly loops around her face. The ridiculous bird clock chirps eight times. Mom looks over at it and her eyes go wide, as if doubting the Eastern Bluebird's song.

"Shit, I gotta get ready!" Taking one last puff of her cigarette, she smashes it into a freshly cleaned ashtray before grabbing her purse and rushing up the stairs. Her bedroom door slams behind her.

I haven't seen her in such a hurry in a while and I'm pretty surprised she wasn't out of breath. It's amazing how the attention of a new man can totally change her attitude. Even if he gives her crumbs, she'll be happier with a man in her life. As long as she thinks she's not alone (I hardly count), Mom's an entirely different person.

Fifteen minutes later, she flies down the stairs with a fresh coat of makeup and a heavy smell of Aqua Net. Her hair is teased, her lips are crimson, and her too short skirt is paired with a ridiculously skimpy crop top. Save for looking like a middle-aged hooker, she's not half bad.

Yanking her car keys from the coffee table, she dashes to the door, not even looking back when she yells, "I'm meeting Tom for drinks. Don't wait up!" The front door slams and I'm alone again.

I could get used to this.

Before I jinx it, I feel like I should cross my fingers and kiss rosary beads, even though I'm not Catholic. Maybe she was too wasted last night to remember our fight. It's a huge relief, but I'm pretty sure I just used up the last chunk of luck I had left.

I turn the lock behind her, knowing full well I'd better savor every drop of peace she just gave me tonight. Surprisingly, my heart beats with a little less hate for her.

I flop onto the sofa, thinking about the house again, thoughts about luck becoming less important. Anything I find out will be fascinating, especially after what Brad mentioned earlier. He did seem reluctant to answer my questions even though I'm pretty sure he thinks the stories are mostly rumors. He was obviously bothered by something.

It's not very late but I head to my room, ignoring the forgotten pile of washed, unfolded clothes in a mound on my bedroom floor. I'm too tired to deal with any more chores tonight and still have a geography quiz I need to study for. I take the folder from my backpack, accidentally catching my watch on one of the side pockets. My wrist is still bruised from Mom's iron grip so I gently pull the buckle back, loosening the strap to set it on the dresser.

Pulling back the covers, I climb in, trying to fold my pillow to make it more comfortable for studying. I lie back, scooting down to settle in, but can't concentrate on my notes. I've had a headache since I got home. I didn't notice it as much when I was busy.

The good thing is, Mom pretty much has a pharmacy in her medicine cabinet. I'm sure I'll find something. I hate taking pills but I'm going to make an exception tonight. I need to sleep and shut off my brain. If I take something now I can study for another thirty minutes, which gives me plenty of time to review my notes, and then hopefully drift off into a wonderful, dreamless sleep.

Her room reeks of smoke and Aqua Net. Turning on the overhead light, something sitting on her nightstand catches my eye. It looks like a picture. As I get a little closer I immediately realize what it is and pick it up. My stomach drops and I let go, watching the photo fall to the floor. It's an old, black and white picture of the Emory house.

A thousand thoughts begin swirling around in my head. What the hell is it doing in my mother's room? Did she put it there? Are we related to the Emory family? I cautiously reach down and pick it up, gingerly, like it's going to explode in my hands, and study it for several minutes. The house looks different, somewhat new, even though it's in black and white. But it's definitely the same house.

I turn it over and see the handwritten words: *Emory, 1910.*

My heart is beating so fast I need to sit down or throw up, I'm not sure which. A feeling of dread hits my body and I run back to my room, slamming the door behind me.

Still holding the picture, I pull the blankets over myself and sink back down. As if doing so will make everything better.

And, it does.

Sort of.

I have no idea what to do next and have so many questions I can barely think straight. How did it get there? Where did it come from? Why would she have it? What's the connection?

It makes no sense.

Finally, after several minutes, my heart slows down, allowing me to relax even with the headache I forgot to take something for. I have no idea when, or if, Mom will be home tonight to even ask her about the picture. I'm not sure I'll be able to stay awake long enough to wait for her. But I'll try. I need to know.

I'm so startled by a loud, buzzing sound that I nearly fall off the bed and out of an amazing dream. Blinking my eyes to clear the sleep-fog, I realize it's the alarm clock and slam my palm down on the snooze button. No telling how long it's been going off; I usually catch it beforehand. I've trained myself to wake up on my own and only have it set for insurance. I just hope Mom didn't hear it. She sleeps like a post-traumatic stress victim, bolting up at the slightest sound. Even dead drunk, she's more alert than anyone sober.

I dreamed I was at the Emory house as it is in the photograph. This time the inside was totally different—not empty or abandoned like it is now. There was also a guy, someone young like me with the most mesmerizing emerald green eyes. They were almost transparent, like the color had a will of its own. They captivated me and I'm pretty sure I couldn't have stopped looking at them if I tried. Other than the shape of his face, his eyes were all I could see, and every second that goes by I have a yearning in my gut to go back. It's like an invisible rope is physically pulling on my heartstrings and on every bone and muscle and cell in my body, and I have to go.

Now.

I grab the first piece of clothing I see on the floor and give my hair a quick brush. Jerking my watch off the dresser, I suddenly feel another intense pull. Only this time, it's way stronger, like whatever's causing this is getting impatient.

What the hell?

I can't leave fast enough and even skip checking myself in the mirror. The house needs me and I don't have a choice but to do what it wants.

CHAPTER ELEVEN

WITHIN A MATTER of minutes I can see the house. I have to stop for a second and catch my breath, flushed with exertion and relief, but I barely get more than a few seconds. The extreme wrench in my gut is back with a vengeance and the need to keep going consumes me all over again. It's beyond strange, even a little frightening, but I don't have time to think about it—I *have* to get inside.

Glancing in both directions, I dart across the street, hoping no one sees me. Thank God it's pretty much a ghost town this early in the morning, the light from the sun barely peaking over the horizon. I have no doubt I look like a lunatic, that crazy girl on her way to a house, rumored to be haunted.

I run as fast as I can to the window, the same window that completely changed my life. I nearly trip when I sprint through, almost landing on the disgusting mattress. I couldn't see it until now because it's so dark but there's just enough light for my eyes to adjust. I scan the room and my first thought is to call out, announcing to the house that I'm here, but somehow, I'm sure it already knows.

Creepy.

Taking in a few deep breaths, I steady myself against the wall, wishing my body would stop shivering.

"Hello?" I call out, panning from one side of the room to the other.

There's only silence, but I'm grateful to have more control over my emotions again.

I'm just about to call out again when a door shuts in another room, practically making me jump out of my skin. I don't have that good feeling like before. It's really cold in here, colder than it is outside. I'm starting to doubt why I'm even here and consider making a run for it.

"Candice," a male voice whispers.

My eyes go wide. I try but fail to see where the voice came from. The only thing I know is that this time it isn't my imagination.

The room is still too dark to see much, which makes hearing my name even scarier. I start to tremble, then full-out shake when I hear a door open with a long, slow creak. I instantly understand why people pee their pants when they're terrified.

"Do not be afraid," the voice says.

"Oh my God!" Something touches my shoulder and I yelp, just before a wave of calm washes over my body. It's as though my panic button has been switched off.

"Much better," the same voice whispers in my ear.

The close proximity of his breath to my ear should've made me scream, but I only want to hear it again. I need to hear that beautiful voice again.

"Please," I softly beg. "Don't go."

I whip my head to the right when I see movement. Without thinking, I clasp a hand to my mouth as I watch a shadowy mist rise inches away.

"You must trust me."

His beautiful voice is all around me again and the amazing feeling is back. I close my eyes automatically because his voice sounds like the most incredible music I have ever heard—all I want to do is take it in.

Something isn't right.

It feels like I'm playing tug-of-war with my mind, fighting my own survival instinct to run. Everything about this is wrong. I can feel it gnawing at my insides, but I can't get enough of this euphoria.

Bending my knees, I'm able to slowly ease down into a sitting position. Hopefully, the more submissive I am the less likely I'll be murdered.

I keep scanning the room but there's no hint of him or the black mist. Somehow it vanished as easily as it rose.

"You will only see me when I wish it."

Again, I nearly leap out of my skin. His voice resonates with a soft echo, like we're in some kind of canyon. I'm shaking again and my fear overrides the calm I just felt.

The silence in the room is deafening. The crickets chirping loudly just ten feet away outside the window seem like they've been muted. My mind keeps playing tricks on me because I think I hear footsteps. Or maybe it's the wind hitting the house. I can't be sure.

Practicing my breathing, I'm suddenly gifted another dose of relaxation with what feels like a hand on my shoulder. This time I'm a little more prepared. I don't jump or call out, only close my eyes while my body is soothed all over again.

I'm so relaxed I'm no longer afraid to ask him a question. "Who are you?"

There's a pause before he says, "My name is Atticus." *Oh. My. God.*

I look up, leaning in the direction of his voice, but can't make out a clear picture of his face. Now the shadows are playing tricks on me.

"I d-don't..." Stumbling for words, I stop in mid thought, trying to unscramble my head.

"I have chosen you," he whispers.

I see him walk out of a corner shadow that kept him hidden and I'm completely enthralled. He lifts his head, revealing emerald green eyes that seem to actually glow in the un-lit room. Those same mesmerizing eyes from my glorious dream.

"I-it was you." I pause to catch my breath. "In my dream."

The way he looks at me answers my question.

"I will not harm you." His hand takes mine and I look down to see white, perfect skin that's cool to the touch.

"I don't understand," I admit, hoping I don't start to hyperventilate when another burst of calm washes over me. How he's doing it, I don't care because I'm starting to want more every time. This is better than any medicine.

"You may ask me anything," he says, still holding my hand.

"Are you homeless?" I ask, hoping I don't offend him.

"No," he simply says, looking away.

The shadows move across the wall, away from me as if agitated by my interrogation, but I keep going.

"How could you have been in my dream? Why do I feel like we've met before?"

He turns back to me, giving me another glimpse of his beautiful eyes. It seems like he wants to tell me more. "I am capable of more than you can imagine," he admits after a slight sigh.

"Like reading minds?" I blurt out, like someone who just figured out a riddle.

His lips curl into a smile and I immediately feel a warm pulse between my legs. "Something like that, yes."

CHAPTER TWELVE

WHERE THE HELL *am I?*
My eyes flash open and I'm about to scream when I realize it wasn't real. It was a full-on nightmare. I was standing on a banister with my neck in a noose. I was about to jump. I was dreaming. *Dreaming.* But it felt so real I think I might throw up.

A beam of sunlight blinds me, making it impossible to see anything.

No, no, no!

My eyes dart around the room. I touch my watch, scooting over the second I see a dark spot, still groggy from sleep. I catch a glimpse of the time, but I must be reading it wrong. I probably need another second for my eyes to adjust. Checking it again, the air is sucked out of my body.

Holy shit.

There is no way it's 3:23 in the afternoon. A split second later, my stomach plunges in a downward spiral of nausea.

What.

Is.

Going.

On?

I jump up, pulling my body off the floor, but have to catch my balance from the instant head rush. I can't give it a second thought as panic overrides everything. How can this have happened again?

Without thinking, I bolt through the window like I'm being chased by a pack of rabid wolves, pounding the pavement fast and furious to get as far away from that crazy house as I can. Once again, hours have escaped me and I have no memory of falling asleep. The only thing I remember is the intense need to get back to that house. I've somehow missed an entire day of school and classes and *shit*, even a geography quiz.

But wait. I stop when I come to a corner a few streets down. Was he real or was he just in my dream?

"Atticus." I say his name out loud and a surge of warmth, almost like arms, wraps around my body. I close my eyes because it feels good, like that euphoric sensation I get when I'm in the house. I know it's wrong somehow but it doesn't matter. It feels so good I don't want to question it.

"Candice?" a voice calls my name.

Startled, I open my eyes and see Brad walking toward me with a puzzled look on his face.

Shit, shit, shit!

Something in the pit of my stomach tells me to run but I breathe in, waiting for it to pass. I don't want him to think I'm completely crazy.

"Hey," I say, too freaked out to form any other words.

"I came by to pick you up this morning but no one answered the door. Are you sick?"

The genuine worry blanketing his face cuts at my heart so I turn away, trying to think of something better than the truth. Anything other than admitting I fell asleep in that amazing, scary, wonderful boarded up old house.

"I uh...yeah, wasn't feeling well," I lie.

He scans me up and down and suddenly I realize I don't have on any makeup and I don't recall what I'm wearing, but I'm sure I look ridiculous. Never the way I want him to see me, but it might work to my advantage. And right now, I just want to get home before I have a panic attack.

"Oh, okay," he says, shoving his hands in his pockets.

I think we're both uncomfortable, but clearly for very different reasons. When his eyes scan me one last time I'm pretty sure he really does think I look like a crazy person and God help me, I'm also not wearing a bra.

Perfect. Go ahead and run, Brad. Here's your chance.

He cocks his head, squinting his eyes with a look of confusion and says, "Why aren't you home?"

And there it is. The question I was hoping to avoid. The one I don't have a good answer to. Well, nothing he'd understand, anyway, because telling him the truth isn't even an option. So I lie again, but not entirely.

"I needed some fresh air."

Brad looks away, as if contemplating what to do next and says, "C'mon, I'll drive you home."

Thank God his interrogation is over, but I feel like shit for lying to him.

"My car's just over there." He points to the gas station across the street.

"No, it's okay. I can walk," I answer, folding my arms to keep my boobs from bouncing around.

"C'mon, Candice. Just let me take you home." He flashes me a crooked smile and of course, I'm a goner. Again.

It's awkward as hell as we walk side by side in total silence but once I get over the shock of seeing him, it feels good to have him close. I'm breaking my own rules around him left and right, and I'm starting not to care.

"Hey, Brad!" a female voice calls out from behind us.

We turn around at the same time, like someone just caught us stealing a six-pack. I'm completely mortified for anyone to see me like this but clearly, that ship has sailed.

"Oh, hey, Sarah," Brad says back, grabbing my hand as he picks up the pace.

I recognize her. She's the same girl I saw in the hall who gave me the dirty look when I was walking with Brad. And here I am again, walking with him.

"Aren't you going to introduce us?" she asks, quickly catching up to us.

Brad stops and lets out a deep breath, then turns to me, placing his hand on my lower back. "Sarah, this is Candice. Candice, this is Sarah."

It's clear that his introduction was meant to be quick, as he hurries to open my car door.

"Well, doesn't she have a last name?" Sarah asks in a sing-song voice. Sarcasm must be her specialty because her tone is drenched in it.

"Stop it, Sarah," Brad spits back.

It doesn't take a rocket scientist to see he's not enjoying this conversation.

She moves closer, leaning into his chest while her long, red nails slowly glide down, just touching the top button of his jeans. Brad grabs her wrist with lightning speed, pulling it away.

"C'mon, Bradley. Don'tcha miss me?" She whispers in Brad's ear but I can hear every word and I'm pretty sure she's very aware of that fact.

Holy shit, who does this?

"I said stop it, Sarah," Brad snaps back, biting out his words, looking at me the whole time.

"Why don't you take your little friend home and meet me back at my place so we can talk? You know, somewhere private." Sarah smiles and then narrows her eyes directly at me. She smirks like she's won Brad back.

Her confidence is freaking amazing, I'll give her that. But I also want to slap her across the face.

"We broke up two months ago. There's nothing to talk about." Anger contorts Brad's face, turning it almost blood red as he holds her wrists away from him.

"Who says we're gonna talk, sweetie?" Her syrupy voice drips with condescendence, like she's all of a sudden talking to a child.

Ick.

Brad doesn't answer and pushes back, letting go of her. Her face changes and I can tell she's shocked he choose crazy-dressed-zero-makeup girl over her.

Under normal circumstances, I'd agree with her. I must look ridiculous in my purple sweatpants and light green tank top (sans bra), but it clearly doesn't matter to Brad. He heads straight for me and takes my hand before gently gesturing me into his car. I watch him take one last look at Sarah, narrowing his eyes as if sending a message not to screw with him. She smiles back, apparently unaffected, and I catch her sneer directly at me before Brad pulls away.

Holy shit.

I'm convinced if she had the superpower to kill someone with a look, I'd be bleeding out in Brad's hand-me-down Porsche.

I have no idea what to say. Do I acknowledge whatever *that* was? Do I change the subject? I almost feel sorry for him because he was clearly pissed. Even embarrassed. And what was even crazier—as ridiculous as I must look, Sarah was the one causing trouble.

Out of nowhere, a sharp pain hits me as Brad shifts into first gear, pulling out of the gas station. I have to suck in a breath to keep myself from crying out. Prickling, sharp pins and needles poke their way up and down my back, almost as if telling me that sitting here is exactly where I shouldn't be. Like I'm being punished. I turn to look at him but he doesn't seem to notice. He still looks really upset about what just happened.

Impossibly, the pain is getting worse and I can feel my body start to tremble. Tucking my hands under my legs, I look away from Brad, trying like hell to fight it.

What is happening to me?

"Hey, sorry about Sarah." Brad looks over at me, rubbing my arm. "She thinks she owns me."

"It's okay—I think I just need to go b-back to b-bed," I manage to say, but it's hard to think straight.

"Are you okay?" He pauses, as if choosing his words carefully. "I'm not interested in her, you know." He takes my hand again, rubbing his thumb across my hand as if apologizing through touch. My pain finally begins to fade.

Thank God.

In a matter of seconds he's turning down my street and I'm instantly happy he paid enough attention yesterday to remember where I live. A benefit of a small town.

"Thanks for the ride." I smile, silently praying the pain is gone for good.

He gives me another concerned look and says, "Candice, talk to me."

"About what?" I ask, knowing he wants to settle the Sarah thing.

"I'm seriously not into her." He gives me a pleading look, making me almost forget the pain I just suffered through.

"It's okay," I say, locking eyes with him. "Besides, it's none of my business."

Still holding my hand, he pulls me close, kissing my temple before whispering, "Yeah, it kind of is."

I'm not going lie, I like what I'm hearing, even though I'm pretty sure this relationship (or whatever it is) is probably doomed before it even gets started. Not to mention my obsessive fascination with a beautiful man living in an abandoned house. I'm not sure if I'm losing my mind or hormonal, but right now my head is spinning.

"Thanks, I have to go," I say, squeezing his hand before letting it go because it's all I can give him right now. Hopefully, it's enough. I need to process what happened today. If I don't get some answers soon, I'm going to end up in a mental hospital.

His face drops like he just lost his last friend. "I'll pick you up tonight at seven if you're up for it."

"Oh." I pause because he's still looking at me with that face. I totally forgot about going with him tonight. "Okay, yeah, we can still go."

"You sure?" He raises his brows. "You feel well enough to go?"

"Yes, yes, I'm sure." I say back, trying to give him a genuine smile as I run up to my door.

CHAPTER THIRTEEN

~~BRAD~~

CANDICE COULDN'T GET away from me fast enough. Jesus, what the hell was Sarah thinking? I haven't spoken to her in weeks and she pulls that shit? A normal person would move on but she isn't normal and she hasn't changed. She's still the same immature, entitled, over-privileged girl I was stupid enough to date. This is my fault. I should have known when she walked up to us nothing good would come from it. Why didn't I just ignore her and walk away? Either way I looked like an asshole.

Glancing over at the passenger seat, I can still imagine Candice sitting there. Hell, I can still smell her and it's driving me nuts that I don't know what's going on inside her head. When she got out of my car, I realized something. I want to spend as much time with her as possible. But I have to be cool about it because she's almost like a scared animal and I don't want to spook her. It's entirely possible I'll scare her away.

Instead of going home, I decide to drive around to clear my head. I can think in peace without Mom attacking me with questions about my day. I'm pretty sure she thinks I'm still sad about breaking it off with Sarah. I tried to reassure her that I'm okay, but it's like trying to take a bone away from a dog. She'll keep chewing on it until it's gone—at least in her own head.

The school is just up the street so I pull into a parking place and turn up some Van Halen. It's after hours so not a lot of people are around, which is good. I lean my head back on the seat and close my eyes.

I hear three loud knocks on my window and jerk my head to the left. Nick and Paul are standing just outside, laughing as I roll down the window.

"Hey, Sleeping Beauty. Did we wake you?" Nick elbows Paul and they both bust out laughing again.

"You're both fucking hilarious," I say, starting the engine.

"Whoa." Nick pauses as if he's surprised I'm irritated. "What's up your ass?"

"Nothing. I gotta go."

"Hey, wait. Can you give me a ride back to my house?" Nick asks.

"Dude, your house is like four blocks away."

"C'mon, Brad. My legs are sore from lifting and my truck's in the shop."

"You do realize I can only take one of you, right?" I ask as Paul stands there with his hands in his pockets.

"Whatever. Check ya later," Paul shoots over his shoulder as he walks away.

"Thanks," Nick says, already opening the passenger door as he plops down in the seat like he owns it. "Wanna toss the football around?"

"Dude, you smell like shit."

"I just worked out, cut me some slack." He shakes his head, pushing the button to open the window.

"Okay, I've got some time, but I thought you were sore?" I say, hoping anything he says will distract me from obsessing over Candice.

"Dude, I had to get the fuck away from Paul." He pauses, reaching into his pocket for God knows what. "He's being a pussy about some chick and I'm sick of listening to his whiney ass."

I ignore his dig on Paul. I don't even want to go there when it comes to either of their girl issues. "If your truck's in the shop, how are you and Beth getting to the movies tonight?" I ask, hoping he bows out so I can have Candice all to myself.

"Shit, I didn't think about that."

"Don't sweat it," I say a little too fast.

Nick looks at me as he contemplates the problem, then suddenly gets this stupid grin on his face like he's just remembered the code to get into Fort Knox. "Wait, my mom'll let me drive her car, it's all good." He lifts his hand for a high five. "Dude, she's making brisket tonight. You can stay if you want. I love brisket."

I swear the boy has the attention span of a freaking June bug.

"Oh, shit! I meant to tell you—Sarah was asking about you yesterday."

"Awesome." I don't even try to hide my sarcasm. "What did she want?" I ask, not really wanting to know.

"Everything I knew about Candice."

"Fuck." I whip my head in his direction. "What did you say?"

"Nothing! Jesus, don't get your panties in a wad! I only said that she's new and you were helping her find some classes."

"Yeah, Candice and I just ran into her about an hour ago at the Quick Stop. She was being her normal bitchy self, totally making me look like an asshole in front of Candice."

Nick slowly turns his head and looks at me, smiling way too much for my level of comfort. "You really like her."

I roll my eyes. "Yeah, ya dumbass. Why else would I ask her to the movies? Now I'm wondering why the hell I asked you and Beth to come with us."

Of course, that makes him laugh.

I can't help but smile back, which makes him laugh even harder.

Damn him.

"You got it bad," Nick teases, knuckle punching my arm.

"You're such an asshole," I say, pulling into his driveway.

"You keep fucking with me and I'm out of here."

"Okay, okay...Jesus."

Nick is right. I am being sensitive. Candice is practically oozing from my pours and it's freaking me out.

He finds a football in his garage and throws it at me before I'm ready. The ball hits me in the shoulder but bounces up. I catch it with one hand.

"Nice save!"

"Asshole."

Their German Shepard tears into the front yard, wagging its tail and practically climbing up Nick's body as he licks his face.

"Hey, Harvey—how ya doing, old boy?"

Nick takes off in a run and Harvey chases after him to the backyard. I follow, thinking we'll throw a few passes before I head out. I watch Nick play with his dog for a few more minutes when he turns around and leans against the back of the garage. His expression is far away, like he's in deep thought.

"Do you ever think about that night in the old Emory house?" he finally asks.

I kick a few small pebbles the dog knocked out back into the flowerbeds, but try not to think about the Emory house. I don't really want to relive that night.

"Yeah, sometimes. Why?" I admit, a little curious as to why he's asking.

"I don't know. I think that place really is haunted." He looks over at me. "Like everyone says it is."

"Nah. I think Paul just shot off his mouth and someone decided to pull a stupid prank." I lie because I really don't know what happened, but saying it's somehow Paul's fault makes it less real.

"Maybe," Nick adds. "But since no one's given any of us any shit about it at school, ya gotta wonder."

"I don't think about it much. You shouldn't either," I say, hoping he'll drop it.

"Paul said the same thing," he admits.

"For once, you should listen to him," I tell him. "You gonna throw me the ball or what?"

CHAPTER FOURTEEN
~~CANDICE~~

T HE SECOND I shut the door, the flashing light on the answering machine catches my eye. I almost trip on my own feet, trying to get to it before it blinks again. I'm pretty sure I know who left a message before I push play. As soon as I hear a woman's voice, saying she's calling from the school attendance office, I hit erase.

God must be smiling down on me at this moment because if Mom had gotten to that message before me, I'd have hell to pay. I probably won't be as lucky next time. I have to put an end to this insanity. But why is it happening? And why am I dreaming about Atticus? Who is he? Hell, *what* is he? All I know is, he seemed very real this morning and in my dreams. He even told me he has psychic abilities, so maybe there's a way I can talk to him in my sleep.

Assuming he shows up at all.

The front door slams, startling me out of my thoughts. My head automatically turns toward the sound and I see my mother carrying a grocery sack into the kitchen. I suck in a breath and prepare for the worst. It's become a habit since I never know what kind of mood she'll be in. I'm just thankful she doesn't know I skipped school today. Well, sort of skipped, because I didn't mean to.

"Got some food for a couple of days," she says, unloading a bottle of whiskey first.

I leap to her side, pulling out packages of ramen noodles, a can of tuna, and some bread. She likes it when I jump to attention so I do what I know she expects. I submit in every way. It's just easier.

"Make some good tips?" I ask, already knowing the answer since her surprise grocery shopping pretty much confirms it.

"Yeah." She lights a cigarette and plops down on a kitchen chair. "Worked an extra shift."

"You must be tired," I say with more sympathy than I feel.

As if I had reminded her of it, she pushes back the chair and grabs the two packs of menthols that were tossed on the table. Her other hand reaches for the fresh bottle of whiskey as she walks out of the room without saying word.

No telling how her date went last night, but I'm not going to open that can of worms. I'm just relieved when I hear her door shut. Another potentially volatile situation averted with a little kiss-ass and fake sympathy.

Check.

~ ~

Tying back the curtains, I open my bedroom window and stand in front of the makeshift vanity I created out of an ironing board I found next to the dumpster and an oval mirror I nailed to the wall. It turned out better than I thought and gives me tons of room to spread out my makeup.

Brad will be here in less than an hour, so I need to tell Mom I'm going out. There's no way I'll mention anything specifically about Brad because not only will she give me the third degree about him, she'll also want me to introduce them. And I can't do that. I won't take the chance that she'll be so wasted her words won't come out right. That's almost more embarrassing than her drunken stagger. Hopefully since she worked a double shift she'll be too tired to really care. But just in case, I'll also leave her a note. I've learned it's never a bad idea to cover all my bases with her.

Pressing the side of my face up to her door, I can't hear anything, so I knock softly incase she's sleeping.

"Mom?" I whisper. "Got a minute?" Turning the knob, I peek my head past the slightly opened door.

"Yeah, what do you need?"

She's lying down on her bed with the back of her hand across her forehead.

"You okay?" I ask, still whispering.

She looks over to me. "Got a headache and my feet are killing me."

"Sorry. Do you need anything?" I ask, knowing a little kissing up will only help.

"No, I already took something. What do you want, Candice?"

"Oh, a few friends from school invited me to go to the movies with them tonight."

"Well how freaking nice. How are you gonna to pay for it?"

Crap, I didn't think of that. I'm pretty sure Brad will be paying since he asked me but I don't dare tell her the truth.

"I still have some birthday money left over," I say, hoping the whisper in my voice somehow shrouds my deception.

She narrows her eyes. "It's a school night, I don't think so."

"Please, Mom? I promise I'll be home by curfew."

"You know I don't like you going out on weeknights."

I don't answer right away because I don't want to get into an argument. That's when things go bad. But I need to think of something. I decide to change the subject. Maybe I can soften her up.

"How'd your date go with Russ?" I smile, stepping into the room.

She gives me an eye roll. "Oh, he's a dumbass. But he has money so I'll be nice to him."

I chuckle like I approve of her taking advantage of him. It's not the worst thing she's ever done. "Hey, there's no law against being nice," I say, still smiling as I grab the blanket at the end of the bed and drape it over her. "It's a little chilly in here."

She leans over and lights a cigarette, exhaling the smoke out of the side of her mouth. "What time does the movie start?"

Bingo.

"I'm not sure." Even though I am. "I think about eight. We might eat, too," I lie.

She takes another drag from her cigarette, squinting her eyes from the smoke.

"Be home by midnight." Then points her finger at me. "And not a Goddamned second after."

"Okay, thanks, Mom," I say, closing the door softly. *That was easy.*

Almost too easy, but to be safe, I'll still leave her a note.

After freshening up my makeup and curling the ends of my hair, I grab a pen and piece of notebook paper from my backpack. *Out with friends to the movies,* I write. *Be back by midnight.*

No *love, Candice* or silly little hearts because even I can't fake those. Still holding the note, I pull the strap of my purse across my chest, tossing in a few leftover coins, some lip gloss, and my I.D. I take one last look at myself in the mirror before closing my window and heading down stairs.

I flip on the kitchen light, startled when I see a black roach scamper across the counter, immediately making me cringe. I can't stand bugs, especially disgusting roaches.

We don't have enough food lying around to attract them so they must be coming from some other apartment. I'm so grossed out, I tiptoe into the kitchen like I'm walking through a minefield. I take Mom's note and fold it in half, leaving it upside down on the table like a little tent so it'll catch her eye in case she wakes up and doesn't remember where I am.

I shut off the light and wait for Brad by the door. He'll be here any minute but I don't want him ringing the bell or knocking too hard. I can't allow anything or anyone to screw up how smoothly things have been going. I just want this one night to go well. Without any embarrassment from Mom.

At 7:03, I hear Brad's Porsche and wait until I hear his footsteps climbing the stairs before I open the door.

"Hey." I can't help my huge smile because, holy crap, he looks hot.

Brad's face brightens up the second he sees me. "Hey. Everything okay?"

"Oh, yeah, my mom isn't feeling well. I figured it would be quieter this way."

"Makes sense," he says, reaching for my hand. "You look nice. Ready to go?"

"Yes."

I like that he took my hand and didn't make me feel weird for opening the door the second he got here. Even though I've only allowed him to see the parts of me poking out on the surface, I'm starting to feel like I can be myself with him. No eggshells. No tiptoeing. It's nice to be able to relax and be with someone who probably gets me better than anyone has in a long time.

The theater must be *the* teenager hangout because it's completely covered with them. I feel like I'm at school all over again only this time, it's nighttime and no one is being watched by an adult at the front of the class. Brad keeps his hand on mine, leading me through the maze of people outside. He opens one side of the double doors for me to go through first. Almost immediately, a guy as tall as Brad, wearing a backwards ball cap, walks up to us and punches Brad in the shoulder. The girl next to him is already looking me up and down.

"Dude, where you been all my life?" The guy with the hat says.

"Hey." Brad glances down at me and I smile, trying not to look nervous. "Candice, this is Nick and Beth."

She finally looks me in the eye when I say "hi" and her bitchy expression morphs into a bitchy smile.

"Here," Nick says, handing Brad something. "They were almost sold out, so I bought the tickets."

"Thanks," he says, taking our tickets and handing me one. "You and Beth wanna grab us some seats?" He squeezes my hand and winks. "I'm on popcorn duty."

"Sure." I smile back, dreading that I have to be alone with her. I'm a pretty good judge of character and can already tell Brad wasn't kidding. She really is a trip. Or maybe just a bitch. Either way, this is going to be interesting.

I look down at my ticket. I never even asked what movie we were coming to see. *Wayne's World.* I let go of Brad's hand and follow the crowd into the theater. I don't even look to see if Beth is behind me but I catch a glimpse of her when I spot four seats together three rows up.

"There." I point, looking over at her.

"Can't you find something closer?" she asks, her cynical expression already pissing me off.

"Go ahead." I point to other seats. "We don't have to sit together."

"Oh," she replies, like I've surprised her.

Does anyone say no to this chick?

"This is fine, I guess." She lets out a deep breath and looks over at me.

I'm not sure she knows my smile isn't quite reaching my eyes and I don't care because Brad and Nick are already walking toward us.

That was quick, thank God.

Brad takes the seat next to me and I'm stuck sitting next to grouch girl, who looks like she could murder every female who accidentally glances in our direction. I think she might even have homicidal thoughts towards me—me, who came with another guy. I have to admit I'm getting a pretty big kick out of it trying to hide my smile before the movie even starts.

Brad must have noticed my giggles and leans close, stretching his arm around me. He turns his head and whispers in my ear, "What's so funny?"

Just the fact that he asked makes it hard not to burst in to laughter and I'm seriously about to lose it. My shoulders start to shake and now he's laughing because it's obviously contagious when I finally manage to whisper back, "Beth." I have to pause and control myself or get caught by pissed-off-jealous-girl. "She's about to go off on the next chick who even accidentally turns her head towards us."

Brad cranes his neck, looking over at Nick, who's obliviously watching the previews, and then says to Beth, "Want some popcorn?" as if trying to divert her attention. It was sweet of him, I'll give him that. Unfortunately, it's pretty clear Beth's not the kind of girl who would notice. She's already too mad at everyone else to care.

She turns her head slowly to look over at him and curtly crosses her arms. She even huffs, like she's a pouting five year old. That's all it takes and I laugh out loud. I couldn't stop myself if I tried. This is pure entertainment. Her eyes instantly shift to me but luckily, I'm able to pass it off like I'm laughing at a preview.

Lord have mercy. This poor girl is a mess.

Suddenly, I don't feel so crazy.

The movie starts soon after and I can't help a little internal sigh as Brad takes my hand. I snuggle next to him and watch Wayne and Garth play air guitars and fantasize to Dream Weaver in Wayne's parents' basement.

~ ~

As we exit the theater, Nick turns to Brad and stops, holding up the line of people behind us. "Dude, I heard there's gonna be a kegger in that field past farmer Black's pasture. Wanna go?"

Brad looks down at me and his lips curl up. It's clear he wants to go, and even though I have no idea what a "kegger" is, I nod anyway, hoping I'm not going to regret this decision.

Minutes later, Brad is holding my hand, occasionally glancing over at me as we follow Nick in his mom's Grand Am.

"You sure you're okay with this?" he asks.

"Yeah," I reply. "But I'm not positive..." I lift my hands and air quote, "what a kegger is."

He laughs. "Oh, it's just a keg party."

"Ah, I figured. So I guess the extra syllable makes it a party?" I tease him, watching the barbed wire fencing light up as we drive by.

"Yeah." He laughs again. "I guess it does."

We stop because Nick pulls over on the side of the road and jogs toward us. Brad lowers his window when Nick gets close.

"Help me with the gate?"

"Sure." He takes a quick glance at me. "Be right back."

I watch them head over to the gate, a little nervous to be alone in the boonies when it's pitch black outside. I'm relieved that it's only a few seconds before Brad is back in the car, following Nick down a grassy pathway. We slow down when we approach two trucks parked side by side with their overhead floodlights on. The area is totally lit up and I can already see at least fifty people standing around holding red Solo cups.

People.

And they're everywhere.

Great.

After Brad parks the car, he comes over to my side and opens my door. I instantly recognize Van Halen's "Right Now" blasting from the truck's speakers.

I smile up at him as he laces his fingers through mine, his hand noticeably warmer because my nerves are already kicking in.

He pauses as if he knows somehow and says, "Don't worry, I'll protect you." Then he grins. "C'mon, let's get a beer."

His warm, firm grip leads me straight into the music and chaos.

Twenty minutes later, I'm holding one of those red Solo cups (full of lukewarm beer) as I watch Brad socialize with ease. My hand is still in his and there's a certain beauty in the way he's able to make me a part of his world even though he's doing all the talking. He makes me want to be here as much as he wants to be and I'm in awe of him all over again. He's introduced me to countless people as they welcome me into their Parkview High kegger society.

The simplicity of the moment is an epiphany for me.

I'm falling for him.

Hard.

~~

Almost an hour has gone by when Nick and Beth eventually join the circle of people surrounding Brad and me. They disappeared a while ago and I was starting to wonder if they'd gone. When I get a closer look, I see that Nick's shirt is buttoned wrong and the back of Beth's hair is a knotted mess with pieces of grass in it. Nick keeps scratching his chest between sips of beer while Beth looks like she's pissed at the world. I try to hide the smile forming on my face by looking down but it's no use. Brad notices and excuses us from the group.

"What are you laughing at now?" he asks, grinning back.

I tilt my head toward Nick and Beth and stifle a laugh. It doesn't take a genius to know what they've been up to. Brad bursts out laughing this time, almost spilling his beer on himself as he leads us several steps away because apparently he needs more privacy to wail his ass off.

"Why the hell..." Laughter takes Brad's breath away for a second. "Why the hell didn't they use his mom's car?"

I can't breathe or look at him because he's making me laugh so hard tears are falling down my cheeks. I have no doubt that by now none of this is subtle, even though we're a good distance away. Of course, Nick and Beth notice and start heading toward us. I do my best to get Brad's attention but it's too late. Brad sees Beth's hair again and it's all over.

"Dude." Nick punches Brad in the arm. "What the fuck is so funny?" He looks at me as if I'm supposed to stop Brad from bellowing his guts out.

It takes a few more seconds but finally, Brad gains control. "Have you seen yourselves?"

Nick looks over at Beth, who's already looking at him, and says, "Oh shit, I thought I got all the grass out." He starts picking at Beth's hair, but she bats him away. Her hands touch the sides of her head and her eyes go wide.

"Are you fucking kidding me?" she snaps at Nick as her hands begin frantically feeling around for pieces of grass.

Now, the three of us are trying not to lose it. Beth looks at Nick like she's going to kill him, then transfers the death glare to me. While she was finger-combing her hair, I made the very wrong decision to brush off the back of Nick's shirt.

"Get the fuck away from him." Beth spits her words out. Her face changes when we make eye contact and I swear, she's about to come at me.

Holy shit.

"Whoa, whoa, Beth!" Nick puts his arms up between us like he's already breaking up a fight.

"Beth…" I start to say but she interrupts, wedging her way past Nick with her finger pointed only inches from my face.

"You touch him again, bitch, and I'll kick your fucking ass!"

"Seriously? You thought I was copping a feel of your boyfriend?" I don't even try to disguise my sarcasm because this is ridiculous. She is completely out of control.

Suddenly, I hear screaming and see her coming straight for me. All I see are hands until Nick picks her up, carrying her flailing limbs away from me.

I'm totally mortified and embarrassed. I've never come close to getting in a fight, much less over a guy. Nick is still holding Beth back when Brad walks past me. He must have had enough because he gets in Beth's face and when she looks up at him I swear I can almost see steam coming from his ears. "You have some serious fucking issues and I can't believe Nick puts up with your bullshit." His voice is calm, cool, and collected, which accentuates how pissed off he must be.

He glares at her for a few more seconds then backs away and takes my hand.

"We're outta here," he shoots over his shoulder to Nick, who looks completely dumbfounded, like someone just gut punched him. Before I know it, we're in his Porsche, driving down the grassy path.

Long moments pass without either of us saying anything. I look down at my hands, picking at a hangnail and wondering what, if anything, I should say.

His hand squeezes my fingers. "You okay?" he finally asks.

"Yeah."

"Sorry, I told you she was crazy jealous."

"You weren't kidding."

"You hungry?" He keeps looking in my direction, but I know if I look at him I'll see the apology in his eyes. Even though he has no reason to. Still, it hurts to know he's upset.

"No. Are you?"

"I could eat."

I look down at my watch. It's almost eleven forty. I know by the time we make it back to town and stop to eat, it'll be past midnight before I get home. I can't be late again, even though there's a pretty good chance Mom will be passed out from her typical night of drinking.

"I should probably head home—you know, to check on my mom," I lie.

"Sure. I understand," he says, but I can hear the disappointment in his voice.

He doesn't say anything else. He just drives. I look out the window, hoping this awkward moment between us will pass. He takes a right at the last light before we get to the apartment and my heart starts to beat so loudly that I'm sure he can hear it. I hate caring this much. It's not what I had planned but it's too late. I want to make him happy.

And then, we're here.

My heart keeps pounding; I wish I could cut it out of my chest.

"I had a good time tonight." He looks down as if he's embarrassed. "Even though Beth went ballistic."

I turn and catch his brown eyes looking at me. "I did too," I say, touching the side of his face. I need him to know I don't blame him for Beth's craziness. "Besides, I needed to come home anyway. My curfew is midnight."

There's something calming in his smile. When his face lights up, my heart snaps back to a normal rhythm. I can relax and it feels good to know he's starting to have that effect of me.

He leans closer and my lips are on his before I know what I'm doing. I want this. I'm going to tell my head to stop over-thinking every single thing for two seconds so I can enjoy this moment.

Our kiss is gentle and sweet. Nothing more. We're not to the stage of fogging up the windows, especially not right outside so Mom can see, but we definitely want more. I know that much.

"Thank you," I say as I pull away, my forehead resting against his.

"For what?" he says, reaching for my hand.

"For the movie and for making me laugh so hard I almost peed."

CHAPTER FIFTEEN

B RAD ASKED IF he could pick me up in the morning and I told him he could. I also told him he didn't have to walk me to the door because I didn't want to take the chance of waking Mom. As soon as I walk in, I hear his car drive away and I'm relieved I made the decision to walk up by myself. Cigarette smoke practically wafts out at me. I can feel my nose scrunching up the second I race up the stairs, hoping somehow I'll avoid the stench. I make it to my room so fast I wonder if the smoke even knew I was there. I close my bedroom door as softly as I can before yanking up the window and turning on the lamp just below.

The house is very quiet. More than likely, Mom passed out long ago. I could check on her, like the dutiful daughter I'm not, or I could relax and think about my date.

The night couldn't have gone any smoother. So why am I waiting for my world to come crashing down?

I force myself to shake off the feeling and glance over at the clock. I made it home ten minutes before my curfew. Another win. I flop onto my bed, sighing when I think about Brad and our kiss. His skin smelled so good and his lips were sheer perfection. Hands down the best kiss I'd ever had.

God, I kissed him first. But I don't care. It was worth it.

The breeze shifts the curtains back and forth. It smells like fall—that undeniable scent of clean sheets hanging outside to dry. It's funny how smells are like time machines. I'm instantly seven years old, running through the clothesline in our backyard, young and carefree during the time in my life that feels so unreachable now that it's hard to go back without getting choked up. Mom and Dad were still together and I was oblivious to their problems. I was oblivious to a lot of things back then; it was pure bliss. In my mind, I had a stable life and I was happy. But the older I got the more I understood and the less happy I became. So many times I've wanted to go back to being that unaware, blissful little girl.

My thoughts are interrupted when I hear someone call my name. It's not Mom because it sounded too deep. So, I look over to the window, thinking Brad must be pulling another Prince Charming act. I'm slightly disappointed when I see no one there and instantly get a sinking feeling in my gut.

Calm down Candice, it's been a crazy night.

I take a deep breath and decide to ignore it. There's a good chance if someone was outside they weren't calling for me. We have several neighbors. That must have been what it was.

Shrugging it off, I plop down on the bed and open my book to the last page I left off. Mr. Darcy just offended Elizabeth at the dance but her wit is lethal and she tells him off before leaving with her family. She does it with such grace and every time I get to this part, she's my hero all over again. As I continue to read, I suddenly realize my room is getting cold so I push the window all the way down and pull the curtains together. Again, no one's there. It really must have been my mind playing tricks on me; it is late and I might have a slight beer buzz.

Walking over to the closet, I take off my clothes and slip on Dad's old t-shirt. I practically leap onto the bed and snuggle in, happy to get right back to Elizabeth's story when I hear my name in a whisper. This time it's clear but it's not coming from the window. My stomach drops. Something isn't right. I think I know that voice.

Holy.

Shit.

My heart starts to race because I know exactly who it is.

Atticus.

But how is this possible? How can I be hearing his voice when I'm nowhere near the Emory house? Could it be my imagination? Maybe, but there's no way in hell I'm going back there tonight.

Wait a minute, if can reach me here, maybe I can communicate with him, too? But how? I need a plan.

~~

I still can't sleep. It's been hours. I keep trying to will myself to dream about Atticus. There's gotta be a way. Besides, I know he's already tying to reach me, even while I'm awake. Therefore, if he can connect with me, why couldn't I do the same with him? I know he has the answers, I can feel it. I have to find out what the hell is going on and why, when I go inside that house, I keep passing out for hours at a time.

The bright red numbers on my bedside clock say 3:23. They glow in silence, almost mocking me until the three turns into a four. I feel my stomach tighten. I'm not sure what to do because nervousness alone is keeping me awake now.

Then it hits me. Half a cup of beer isn't enough. I need more to relax and hopefully sleep. Mom has a secret stash of booze hidden below the kitchen sink. She doesn't think I know about it—just like her tip money in the Folgers can—but since I'm the only one who cleans around here, that small bottle of vodka she keeps for an emergency might be the answer. Maybe a couple sips will help me relax? Or at least calm me down.

Opening my bedroom door, I tiptoe down the stairs, making my way to the kitchen with barely a sound, which is a miracle because the stairs sometimes creak on the left side. Luckily, the stove light is on. Not having to turn on the big kitchen light somehow feels safer. I bend down to open the cabinet and spot the vodka in the same place I discovered it a few days ago.

Bingo!

Tucking the bottle under my arm, I carefully climb the stairs, keeping my feet on the right side as I dart for my bedroom. I stop to listen for a second, sucking in my breath, before gently closing the door. That was almost too easy. But then I think I hear something and my ear is back up to the door. I let a few seconds go by but don't hear anything, only the sound of my heart beating a pulse in my ears. Mom must be deep in her nightly alcohol-induced sleep.

Thank God.

I open the cap and take a whiff. It reminds me of Mom's breath and I'm instantly revolted. I take a sip anyway, already knowing I'll hate the taste, and I do. It's heavy and hot going down, but I know it will make me relax and keep taking one sip after another.

Before long, a warm sensation swirls in my stomach and I turn off the bedside light, climbing in my bed. Moonlight streams in from the window, filling up the room, and I close my eyes, trying to focus on what I'm about to do.

I take a deep breath in through my nose and exhale through my mouth. I do it three more times because when I'm panicked it always helps. Can't hurt to do it now.

"Atticus." I whisper his name out loud, thinking somehow saying his name will help. The warm sensation in my belly increases, continuing to relax my body. I feel a sudden sense of calmness engulfing me.

"Atticus," I whisper again, closing my eyes as my mind starts to slowly drift. Concentrating seems to help and it becomes easier and easier to give in to the soothing heat in my belly. It feels so good I can't think of anything else…

~~

A white, foggy mist surrounds the edges of my sight, making it difficult to see. I'm confused and a little scared when another blanket of warmth washes over me, relaxing my body as the mist begins to slowly fade.

I immediately recognize that I'm back inside the house and it's somewhat dark, just like it was this morning. It feels very different because when I glance around from room to room, I see furniture, pictures and lamps. Even the windows are decorated and no longer boarded up. It's like I've stepped back in time.

I make my way to what looks like a formal dining room, taking in the luxurious drapes pooling on the floor and the enormous crystal chandelier sparkling over the massive dining table. My eyes pan right and I stop, suddenly drawn to the fireplace mantle. Above it is what looks like a family portrait and as I take a few steps closer, I instantly spot him.

Atticus.

The people within the frame seem almost alive because whoever painted them captured their features with incredible, vibrant colors. I can't help but stare at Atticus. He is absolutely stunning, his amazing eyes just as emerald green as when I saw him in the mist. His resemblance to the man and woman sitting just below him confirms they must be his parents. He's a combination of them both, with his father's hard jawline and his mother's plump lips. There's a girl in the picture as well who's most likely his sister, but she's much younger.

My fingers skim the bottom of the frame, eventually gliding up to Atticus as I admire his dark gray suit and the elegantly wrapped tie framing his folded collar. It's very clear they had wealth because they're all dressed beautifully. I'm pretty sure I could stare at them for the rest of my life, taking in every minute detail. I practically have to rip my eyes away because I'm suddenly pulled toward the staircase. As I turn around and make my way to the banister, I notice the artwork in the carpentry. It's as if I'm on a guided tour of how spectacular this house used to be.

Wrapping my hand around the wooden rail, the sensation of warmth is back, somehow making me feel like I'm being invited to keep going. I cautiously take a step, hoping the stairs won't creak like they do at home and thankfully, they don't. When I get to the top I notice there's enough light coming through a second story stained glass window to see a long hallway with several doors. They're all open except for one. The door I now feel a strong need to open.

Reaching for the handle, I turn the knob ever so gently, stepping inside a beautifully candlelit room. It's filled with the same decadence as the rest of the house, with expensive fabrics and furniture. The candles in the wall sconces glimmer, casting unique shadows along the wall, and just below, the marble fireplace is luminous with flame from what looks like freshly cut wood. It's so completely peaceful and welcoming that I'm overwhelmed and caught off guard when tears start to stream down my face.

"Hello, Candice," a voice calls, stopping me in place as I turn in its direction.

His voice is so beautiful.

My eyes pan the room but he's nowhere in sight. The candle flames wave with sudden movement and I try to follow their direction, darting my eyes from the bed to the window to the tall dresser and back again.

"Hello," I answer, breathless.

It's so quiet, except for the crackle from the fireplace, and strangely, none of this feels wrong. Everything about this is right.

My finger wipes away another tear and I softly sit on the bed, hoping he doesn't make me wait too long. The fire pops and sizzles, mesmerizing my gaze. I sigh in contentment when I feel a hand on my shoulder.

"I am pleased you found me," he says, still impossibly hiding himself from view.

"Me too." I smile, looking down at my hands, hoping he continues to talk to me. "W-why am I so drawn to this house?" I finally get out.

A slight breeze flows around my shoulders, whipping my hair as I feel his cool touch on my arm. It feels so amazing my eyes automatically close.

"Do you want to be here, Candice?"

"Oh, yes—yes I do," I answer quickly, without having to think.

"That makes me very happy. I haven't been happy for a very long time."

I open my eyes when I hear footsteps and then I see him. All of him. Just like in the portrait, he has the same clothes, the same youthful look. His emerald eyes catch mine and suddenly it feels like I would sacrifice everything to never have to leave him again.

"You are beautiful," he says, touching the side of my face and instantly I want his approval.

I can't speak because this house, his voice, my want for more is overwhelming. It's as if Atticus knows when he reaches for my hand, pulling me closer to him, that his touch helps. I feel like I'm looking at a beautiful sculpture and the second I take my eyes away, he will disappear. So I don't. I simply stare at him, completely in awe.

"Do you remember me?" he asks, gazing into my eyes.

"I don't understand," I whisper, finally finding my voice.

He smiles, like he can see into every private piece of my soul. "You will, my darling. You will."

CHAPTER SIXTEEN

"CANDICE, WAKE UP!"

I force my eyes to open and see my mother glaring back at me, her hands shaking me relentlessly.

"Are you deaf? Jesus, you're lucky I didn't slap you out of that dream! Who the hell is Atticus?"

I can hardly think straight enough to process her words. Thankfully, she lets go, leaving white marks on my arm from her tight grip.

"Tell whoever it is at the door to stop ringing the Goddamn bell!" she screams over her shoulder, stomping out of my room.

I quickly push the covers back and look over at the clock. It's seven forty; school starts in twenty minutes.

Shit!

I rush downstairs and look through the peephole. I'm pretty sure it's Brad but I put on the chain before opening the door just in case.

"Hey," Brad says, half smiling like he's guilty for coming over so early.

"Hey."

"Did I wake you?" His brows bunch up, making him look vulnerable, and I immediately feel sorry for him.

"No," I lie. "But I'm not ready yet, you go ahead."

"I can wait. How long do you need?" His handsome grin is back.

Fifteen minutes later I'm sitting next to him in the Porsche, windows down and Pearl Jam blaring through the speakers.

He looks over at me curiously, studying my reaction to the loud music, then turns it down. "Too loud?" he asks.

"No, it's fine," I say, shaking my head.

"Listen, about Sarah." He stops when I touch his arm.

"Never mind her. You know that boarded up old house on Oak Lawn?" I ask, trying to be as nonchalant as I can even though just mentioning it makes my heart start to race.

"Uh, oh yeah—you mean the Emory house?" he says, turning the volume all the way down.

I automatically cock my head to one side. It's weird to hear him refer to it like that even though I know he's mentioned it before. The difference is now the name is sticking with me.

Emory. That must be Atticus's last name.

"There's really not much to tell. It's been abandoned for as long as I can remember. Like I said, the guys and I go there sometimes. Why?"

I must be giving him a strange look because he takes my hand. "We don't ever do anything but sit around. It's not like we knock down walls or spray graffiti all over the place—if that's what you're worried about." Brad pauses and looks away before continuing. "We actually went there recently." He glances back over to me.

"We?" I ask, trying to keep my hands from shaking.

"Yeah, me, Paul and Nick," he says matter-of-factly.

I swallow because my throat is suddenly dry. "I remember you saying something about it. Do you go there a lot?" I ask with as little emotion as I can.

"God, no." He shakes his head.

"Why not?" I smile, trying not to seem overly curious.

"I don't know—that house..." He stops himself, then continues, choosing his words carefully. "It's—well, supposedly it's haunted. You know, by the guy who died there." His eyes jerk back at me like he's expecting me to laugh because he's suddenly bat-shit crazy.

"Haunted? Really?" I swallow, knowing Brad's right but slightly relieved that I'm not completely insane either. Atticus is more than just someone I dream about.

Holy shit, I can't breathe.

"Hey, you okay?" he asks, pulling into a parking spot.

"Yeah," I answer, pushing the car door open as I take a deep breath. "I just need some air."

I practically run over to the side of the school building and stand against it, pressing the bricks cool beneath my palms. It's helping because I don't feel like I'm about to hyperventilate anymore. That was close.

Brad catches up to me and by his expression I can tell he's concerned. "I shouldn't have taken you out last night," he says soothingly. "You're still sick."

"I'm fine, really," I lie, hoping it makes him stop with the pity.

"They're just stories, Candice. People just say it's haunted. Nobody really believes it is." His eyes go soft, as if he's talking to a homeless animal in the middle of traffic. "It's just an old abandoned house and nothing more."

I have to admit, he's probably the sweetest guy I've ever met. No one's ever genuinely given a shit. Even the couple of guys I dated before we moved here never cared like him. Probably because I stopped seeing them before they could get too close. But there's something about Brad, something that makes me want to be with him, but letting go and giving someone else control of anything in my life, especially my heart, is something I've never allowed. And now he's looking at me the way every girl wants a guy to look at her. But I'm still having a hard time understanding why.

"You know, you could have any girl you want in this school..." He stops me in mid-sentence and gets really close, so close I can smell the soap he used to wash his face. I look down and watch his lips curl up into his usual sexy smile and his entire face lights up. All it would take is a couple more inches and another kiss...and I'd be a goner.

"You seriously don't get it, do you?" he asks, placing his palm on my cheek. "And the really sucky thing is the bell's about to ring so I can't take the time to explain... but I want to kiss you so hard right now it hurts."

Before I can say anything he turns his head, placing his other palm on my face, and says, "What the hell."

His lips are on mine so fast I barely have time to catch up. They're soft at first, then press a little harder, his warm hands cupping my cheeks. Our lips move in comfortable unison, slightly opening and closing as he teases me with his gentle tongue. I don't want it to end because it's a hundred times more than our kiss last night. It's different than any kiss I've ever been given because there's something behind it. I'm totally lost in the moment when I think I hear a bell or a moan. I can't be sure and I don't really care.

Next thing I know his lips are no longer on mine. He breaks away, grabbing my hand and quickly pulling me around to the front doors, like he knows I need help regaining full consciousness—and he would be right.

His holds on a little tighter when I try to pull away because we're about to smack into a group of teachers. I'm stuck in the stupor of the just-kissed. For now, I let him have control, winding me around corners and more people as we sprint through the halls. Finally, we make it, coming to a stop just outside our first period class. He smiles down at me, winking as he opens the door. I reluctantly walk in first, swallowing hard as a classroom of heads turn in our direction.

"Shit, we're late," he whispers in my ear. "But damn, it was worth it."

My face feels hot but I make it to my seat quickly. It's hard to believe no one can hear my heart practically pounding out of my chest. When I look over at Brad, he's not winded at all, just smiling at me. It's contagious. I should try to focus, but, Jesus, that kiss.

"Nice of you two to join us," Ms. Barnes says.

I try to ignore the fact that everyone is snickering and staring at us because it doesn't matter. Kissing Brad felt so good. He took his time and the mental escape was glorious. I actually allowed myself to get lost in the moment and didn't think about Atticus or my mother or the fact that my life is so screwed up.

I'm half tuned into the mind-numbing talk of the equator, which divides the earth into the Northern and Southern Hemisphere. I look around the room and notice a few students taking notes and am relieved that Brad and I no longer have the full attention of the entire classroom.

Thank God.

Taking in a deep breath, I begin to relax, but can't help thinking back to our kiss and the way Brad held my face, guiding me with his hands. Just thinking about it sends a warm sensation through my body and I find myself staring out the window, imagining myself in a different life.

In the distance two blackbirds fly in unison, landing on an electric wire as several others join them. They turn their little heads as if talking to one another before flying off again, free to go wherever instinct takes them. Someday I'll be free, just like those birds.

"Earth to Miss. Crawford. I hope I'm not keeping you from something," Ms. Barnes's voice interrupts my thoughts.

And everyone is staring at me again. Even Brad. But at least he's not snickering under his breath.

"I'm sorry, what?" I look up at the teacher, catching her slight eye roll.

"I just asked if you knew the degrees of the Tropic of Cancer and the Tropic of Capricorn?" She slowly smiles, as if she's stumped me.

"Oh, um..." I pause for a second, shoving my fantasy away with the giggling behind me. Luckily, I've always liked maps and I smile because the answer is easy for me.

"The Tropic of Cancer is 23.5 degrees north of the Equator and the Tropic of Capricorn is 23.5 degrees south," I reply, pretending I don't notice her total bitchiness.

"That is correct." Ms. Barnes pauses with a faint look of frustration, then walks closer to my desk. "But let me give you a little advice." She tilts her head slightly as if she's already enjoying what she's about to say. "You've already lost five points off your daily grade for being tardy."

I look up, trying not to give her the satisfaction of showing any emotion.

"Therefore, it would probably be in your best interest to pay attention for the rest of the class."

Her undisguised sarcasm causes the entire class to burst out laughing and I can literally feel the blood rushing to my face—no doubt making it beet red. I can see Brad looking at me out of the corner of my eye but thankfully, he's the only one not laughing.

The remaining forty-five minutes are going to be sheer torture. Not because I was laughed at or that the teacher's a complete bitch, but because my head is all of a sudden killing me. I sink back in my chair and rub my temples, hoping to make the pain go away.

"Candice," a voice whispers in my ear.

Stunned, I look around for the source. The hair on my arms is standing on end and I'm praying Brad is playing a trick on me, but he's still sitting in his chair and everyone else is diligently working on their assignments.

"Candice, come back to me."

I look around again because how can no one hear what I'm hearing? And right then I realize. Atticus's voice can't be heard because it's coming from inside my head.

This cannot be happening!

My head starts to pound, as if he's becoming impatient with me. A few minutes go by and the pain gets a little better but then I hear his voice again.

"Come to me now."

Each word pounds in my head and now I'm becoming angry. It feels like my body is being hijacked. I've got to get to that house before this gets worse. And this time, I'm getting some fucking answers.

Clicking the end of a pen up and down as I bounce my foot under the desk, I do anything I can to keep from coming unglued. The bell can't ring soon enough and when it does, I bolt for my locker.

"Candice, wait up!" Brad calls after me.

I can't talk to him right now.

I don't stop and the fact that I'm moving so quickly at all is a miracle. There are so many people already in the hallway but I manage to break through the crowds with my urgency. It's as if they can feel my anxiousness and let me pass. The pain ebbs and flows as I move and once I reach my locker, a hand touches my shoulder. I stop and turn to the right, looking up at Brad's worried face.

"What's wrong? Are you okay?" The desperation in his voice pricks at my stomach.

"Nothing," I bite out. "I just need to go."

"Don't let Ms. Barnes get to you. Nobody likes her."

Without looking up, I shove my entire backpack in the locker and pull out the Geography homework I need to finish.

"What?" I ask, because I'm not listening to anything he's saying. The pull to get to the house is somehow even more enormous, and it's starting to override the headache.

"Trust me, every person in that class was happy she wasn't picking on them."

"Oh, no." I shake my head. "It's not that."

I can't tell him what I'm planning to do. Or that as soon as I close my locker, I'm going to run like hell to that house. He said the place was haunted, that it was just a story. He won't understand and would probably try to stop me. I need to find Atticus. I need to find out what the hell is going on. That spirit or whatever he is owes me an explanation and I intend to get it.

I glance up at Brad but quickly look down again. The confused look on his face as he watches me stuff my locker is starting to get to me. I want to tell him how much I like him and how much that kiss meant to me, but I can't because every second I wait a sharp pain beats inside my skull.

"Why are you in such a hurry?" he asks.

"I—I forgot to do something." I stumble to whip up an excuse. "I need to get home."

Lame, I know, but I don't have a choice.

"Hang on—are you skipping the rest of the day?"

Shit. I didn't even think about that but I can't worry about it now.

"Yeah, I guess I am." I'll just have to stay after tomorrow and make up the work. I don't have a choice.

"At least let me drive you," he insists.

It's hard to look at him, his face oozing concern and confusion. I care about him and definitely want more, a lot more, but I have no control over what's going on inside my body and have to get to the house, so I lie.

"No, I'm good. Besides, I don't want to get you in trouble," I say as calmly as I can, needles pricking at my gut. Closing my locker, I walk away through the maze of people, waiting until Brad is out of sight before I make a run for it.

"Candice!" I hear him call out to me but it's too late, I can't stop now.

CHAPTER SEVENTEEN

~~BRAD~~

OMETHING'S WRONG, I can feel it—something that must have happened in class. She was fine, and then it was like she was a caged animal, desperate to be freed. But what could it have been? Our kiss? The bullshit Ms. Barnes gave her? I sure as hell don't know. The look on her face was pure determination, like she couldn't get out of here fast enough. She was also stumbling for excuses and I have no doubt she was lying.

She blew right out the door before I could catch her but I'm not far behind. I know she's got to be around here somewhere but when I scan the parking lot, there's no sign of her. I have a bad feeling and rush to my car and start the engine, pulling out quickly as I pan the parking lot one last time. Nothing.

Jesus, did she run the whole way?

I have to slam on my brakes to keep from hitting another car. I'm not paying attention but right now, I don't give a shit. I have to find her and Oak Lawn is most likely the way she would have gone.

I pull onto the street, frantically looking in both directions, trying to catch a glimpse of her as I keep to the right. I'm going five miles an hour so I can inspect every inch of one sidewalk and then the other. Giant pine trees line the road and practically blanket the front lawns of every house, all of them mansions. If you're rich in this town, Oak Lawn is where you live. All the houses are meticulously kept and glorious.

Except for one—the Emory house.

It's been off and on the market so many times I'm pretty sure the local realtors have given up on it. Truth is, nobody wants to buy it because some people in this town believe the ridiculous rumors that it's haunted. People can be superstitious, but I'm not convinced. Yeah, I was scared when I couldn't explain what happened to the guys and me, but that doesn't automatically mean it's haunted. There's a logical answer. There always is.

CHAPTER EIGHTEEN

~~CANDICE~~

I ONLY STOP WHEN the house is in full view. I ran like hell the entire way and have pause to catch my breath. I feel so out of control even though I'm doing everything I can to get to the house. The pull to keep moving is impossibly stronger and my headache is beginning to turn my stomach into knots. It's clear that the longer I wait, the more severe everything becomes.

I manage to look around, hoping like hell no one can see me because I feel like I'm going throw up any second and I don't want anyone to see me puking in their bushes. Thankfully, there's only one car coming down the street, and it's pretty far away. Glancing back at the house, I know I can't wait any longer. I have to make a run for it, to get there before my head explodes or my stomach has time to catch up.

As soon as I cross through the window I scan the room, half expecting Atticus to be standing with his arms folded across his chest, tapping his foot. But he's nowhere in sight. The room looks exactly the way it did the last time I was here, and interestingly, the pain and nausea have completely disappeared. It's a relief to have control over my body again. But now that I've had a chance to recover, I'm pissed, even though that same incredible feeling is back. Somehow I'm able push the euphoria away, which is a good thing because I still don't have any answers. I do know that I'm sick of playing games and I'm sick of feeling like someone's puppet.

Without thinking, I scream, "Atticus!"

I'm met with silence and even though the pain has stopped, the longer I have to wait, the more frustrated I become.

"Atticus, I know you're here. Answer me, Goddammit!"

A slight breeze whips through my hair and I scan around for its source. My eyes catch a glow coming from upstairs and I bolt in its direction, climbing two steps at a time. As I get closer, I see that the light is coming from the same bedroom as in my dream, but unlike then, I seem to have more control over the way I feel.

The door is halfway open and creaks as I walk into the room, breaking the eerie silence still present all around me. A tall, silver candelabra giving a warm, yellowish glow to what would normally be a pitch-black space stands next an ornate straight back chair, which looks to have been intentionally placed.

Okay, I can take a hint.

The silence is almost deafening, so I take a seat, crossing my legs as I rest my arms on the rich, dark wood. I wait for what feels like an eternity. I won't play his games for long. I want answers now, and I'm pretty sure he knows it.

"I'm not going to wait forever, you know," I say, darting my eyes around.

"Hello, Candice." His voice reverberates off every wall.

I flinch, startled by the power of it, but still see no sign of him. I'm spooked but my frustration quickly comes back with a vengeance, festering its way to a boiling point.

"Stop playing games with me! Where are you?" I leap out of the chair, standing with my fists tight at my sides.

A rush of ice-cold air comes from nowhere, causing the candle flames to flicker wildly, as if warning me to back down. I can actually feel his power, so I edge slowly back into the seat. Puffs of cold air escape past my lips as I attempt to calm myself. I'm not used to being hunted by something I can't see.

Something catches my eye and I turn to the right as I see enormous black shadows work their way up one side of the wall, across the ceiling, and back down to the opposite side. Their animal-like shapes distort out from the wall as they creep closer and closer to me. I wrap my arms around my head, hoping I can protect myself before I'm touched.

He's definitely sending me a message.

Then all goes quiet. No movement, no whip of air—nothing. I know I need to keep my cool because without a doubt I've made him angry, but the longer he stays hidden, trying to scare the shit out of me, the more pissed off I become. Using up my last drop of courage, I stand up, turning slowly as I walk toward the door. It's a gamble, but I don't think he'll actually hurt me. So I call his bluff.

"If you're not going to talk to me, I'm out of here," I say with more conviction than I feel.

I reach for the knob and watch it yank away from my grip with such force the door slams, causing the entire room to shake.

"Sit!" he shouts from directly behind me.

I whip around and see him standing in front of the chair, the look in his emerald green eyes making my heart nearly pound out of my chest.

It's him—all of him. And he's magnificent and frightening and beautiful...all at once.

CHAPTER NINETEEN

~~BRAD~~

I SEARCH THE BOTH sides of the street for what seems like hours but is probably only minutes. I think I catch a glimpse of Candice or someone running toward the Emory house but I can't be sure. By the time I realize it might be her, she's gone. Did she go in? Could our conversation have sparked her interest? Why would she stop here if she was in such a hurry to get home? She was clearly bugged about something and the more I sit here, hoping like hell I spot her again, the crazier I feel. I literally just met this girl and can't believe I'm not only running after her, but skipping school to do it. If someone had told me I'd be this insane about a chick I would have laughed in their face. This isn't me. This isn't how I do things. If I were smart, I'd get my ass back to school and forget all about her. It's not like she asked for my help or begged me to come find her. But it's not that easy. I'm falling for her. She's cast some kind of spell on me or has a secret fucking voodoo doll because I can't explain any of this. Sure, she's beautiful and smart and well, amazing, but I've dated other girls similar to her.

That's a lie.

I haven't dated anyone even close to her.

She's real. So much more real than the fake, two-faced girls I do know. She has a certain vulnerability and modest way about her. The way she presents herself attracted me almost more than her beauty. And now, all I know is I'm going to do everything I can to find her.

I probably look like some kind of stalker, staring at the house from my car. It might be better if I pull into the long driveway. The house and surrounding property is large and it looks completely different during the day. More approachable. At night, even the white wood siding seems to take on a different hue. It's as if the house has a mind of its own. I still can't explain what happened the other night when Nick, Paul, and I snuck in. We've come here at least a half dozen times and nothing like that has ever happened before. I even reminded them of it but it was no use, they're both convinced this place is haunted. They're also both idiots. There has to be some kind of explanation because Nick is right, Paul is a pussy, and if he was getting nervous about coming here, there's a big possibility he could have told someone. And they would've had a blast messing with us.

The song on the radio changes and I look down at my watch. Twenty minutes have gone by and there's still no sign of her. Maybe it wasn't her. Maybe she's been home this whole time and I've been sitting here like a dumbass, parked outside this crazy house.

CHAPTER TWENTY
~~CANDICE~~

H IS GREEN EYES are practically glowing. I can't stop looking at them as I make my way back to the chair. Reaching down, I feel around for the armrest and slowly ease into it. The air is suddenly thick, making it hard to get a deep breath, but I can't pull my eyes away from his.

"My temper is quick, but you need not fear me," he says, shifting his gaze away like he's releasing me from his spell.

Blinking to clear my thoughts, I play back what he just said in my head. "It's kind of impossible when you scare me like that," I whisper, trying to keep my voice calm.

As if thinking of his next move, Atticus begins pacing back and forth. The glow in his eyes is dimming. He's right, he definitely has a temper and I should probably keep that in mind. I'm instantly thankful for my years of practice with rage.

Never thought that would come in handy.

He stops and turns his head, staring directly at me, but this time I don't feel trapped in his eyes. "There are things you must learn," he says, his voice cutting through the silence.

As if something clicks in my brain, the question I've wanted to ask him is out of my mouth before I can stop it. "Are you real or are you..." I pause, still trying to comprehend that the man standing in front of me could possibly be something else.

"A ghost?" he finishes.

I nod, studying his every move as he goes back to pacing again. He's wearing the same suit and tie he wore in the portrait and his hands are clasped behind his back. The look on his face is full of concentration. Like he's trying to solve a thousand problems at once. I know the reality of this situation is impossible but my eyes are telling me the opposite. He's real. He has to be.

Then it happens. A wave washes over me and I no longer feel scared or angry. The amazing feeling is back, completely turning my mood.

It's been him all along.

"You did that—didn't you?" I ask, knowing the answer.

"Yes," he replies simply, still pacing.

"So, wait, you're just a figment of my imagination?"

His face changes as he stops mid-stride, stepping toward me. I pull back, hoping he doesn't come any closer.

"Do I look like a figment of your imagination?" His voice almost slices through me.

He's right in front of me, looking as real as anyone else. I can see him breathing and smell the wool in his jacket. I look back up, staring into his amazing green eyes. The eyes that are keeping me mesmerized and suddenly making the blood pulse between my legs.

"No," I say, slightly out of breath.

His lips curl up and I can't speak. My eyes are too busy watching his mouth. I'm completely out of words and totally under his control. And he knows it.

"Take my hand." He reaches out, placing his cool palm in mine, leading us out of the room into the hall-way. We stop at the second story balcony and his grip gets tighter.

What is he doing?

Darkness is beginning to soak up the house and I watch him wave his free hand, instantly brightening the view and transforming the house to its former splendor. It's completely breathtaking, like we've stepped back in time. Gone are the creepy boarded up windows and di-lapidated staircase. In its place are stunning drapes and jaw-dropping woodwork all along the banister. I can even smell wood burning in the fireplace.

"How did you do that?" I ask without thinking, not really expecting an answer.

The house looks exactly like it did in my dream and once again I see the beautiful dining table and brilliant silver candelabra glistening in the flame of candlelight. My breath catches with a kind of split second familiar-ity because it feels like I've been here before, which is impossible.

Atticus turns to me with a peculiar look on his face, as if already reading my mind. "I will tell you every-thing, but you must trust me," he says.

His eyes capture mine again and I'm a goner. I'll listen to anything he has to say. I nod so he'll keep talking. I know it's him making me feel this way but I don't care.

His ice-cold hands take mine and he pauses for a second before saying, "I have been trapped in this house for 104 years." He looks away, as if dreading my reaction.

And he's right because I quickly calculate the numbers in my head and whisper, "104 years ago would be 1888."

Holy shit.

Atticus looks back up at me and I'm instantly relieved by another mental drug rush. The quick pulses of euphoric calm are no doubt keeping me from racing out of here, screaming like a crazy person. He's pretty much confirmed the unimaginable but the more he continues to calm me, the less I care what he says.

He waits, either giving me time to digest what he's just told me or for his latest dose to take effect, I'm not sure which. Maybe he sent me too much this time because for some reason, I suddenly feel exhausted. Too exhausted to stand. Within seconds I'm trying my best to stay awake.

"I need to sit down," I manage to get out.

Another wave of exhaustion consumes me but this time it's way more intense—like Atticus is trying to make me sleep. Why?! My eyelids feel weighted and the more I fight, the drowsier I become.

I must be floating, or maybe I'm being carried; I don't care, because whatever this is, it feels incredible.

~~

I awake later to a quiet room, candlelight flickering on either side of me. I slowly begin to recognize the ornately decorated space as my eyes pan over to the fireplace, with its intermittent crackling of freshly cut wood. I'm still in the house. This is Atticus's room. But where is he? And why did he make me sleep again? Panic rises in my stomach and I have to breathe quickly to get any of air. I'm either dying or hyperventilating and now the room is starting to spin. I jerk up on my elbows, attempting to stop whatever is happening to me.

"Hello, Candice," he says, right on cue, still wearing the same clothes from the portrait. He pauses and comes closer, as if he knows I'm on the verge of a full on panic attack. He raises his hand over my head and then closes his eyes. The panic and struggle for air has been replaced with calm as I take a soothing deep breath.

"Better?" he asks, smiling down at me.

"Yes." I confirm what I'm sure he already knew, but I'm still curious how I got from the top of the stairs to here, so I ask.

"How did I get—"

"In my bed?" I hear his voice, now with laced with a low, almost seductive tone, while his fingers gently run along the side of my face. My eyes go up, and his expression makes me think he's been watching me for a while, and I've just interrupted his fantasy.

"I carried you," he says simply.

"How come I don't remember it?"

"Because you are asleep…it is easier this way."

"Easier for what?"

"For me to communicate with you."

"Oh…" I'm at a loss for words because his beautiful voice is once again resonating outside and inside my entire body and I don't want it to end. Now it's as if every time he speaks, I get a new dose of euphoria. He knows what he's doing and even though it feels slightly dangerous I still don't care. I feel wonderful.

He turns and sits on the side of the bed, placing his hand over mine. With every touch I feel more connected to him. He stops and glances down at me, like he's trying to read my thoughts, and I smile, trying not to discourage him. For some reason I can't allow that.

"May I kiss you?" he asks, the words seeming to have a deeper meaning.

"I would like that," I whisper back.

Without a word, Atticus leans in closer. I can feel the coolness radiating from his skin. He gently places his palm to my cheek, tilts his head, and softly kisses my lips.

They're just lips.

No, they're not.

They're his lips.

His fingers are still laced through mine as he pulls me toward him ever so slightly, but it's like my brain and my mouth aren't mine anymore. Needles deep within the pit of my stomach begin piercing against my flesh, as if my body is sending me warning signals. I try to ignore the discomfort because I don't want him to feel the anxiety festering inside of me. When he pulls away, I look up and smile, attempting to keep my response to the pain as relaxed as possible. If I've learned anything when I'm with Atticus, it's that I have to completely hide my emotions and reactions.

"That kiss is the first of many, my love," he says as he gets up from the bed.

Love? Did he just call me his love?

He walks over to the fireplace and stares at the flame with a faraway look in his eyes.

"I was born in this very room in the year 1868." He turns his head so he can look me in the eyes and I can actually feel his anger. "Twenty years later, I also died here."

His tone immediately changes my mood. I look away, hoping he doesn't suspect I'm starting to freak out again. I need to keep my head clear even though I'm asleep.

This is crazy.

"You do understand that you must keep me a secret?" His eyes glow slightly, as if revealing the severity of his request.

"Of course. There are lots of rumors but nobody would believe me anyway," I say, trying to take breaths between my words.

He notices and narrows his eyes.

"Is there something you are not telling me?"

If this is a dream it's insane how real this feels. I can smell the wax dripping from the candles and hear his voice echo in the room.

"When I was twenty, I fell in love. She was the love of my life..." He pauses. "But I lost her." He looks down, his grief still raw. "Her name was Josephine."

I'm caught off guard because I didn't expect to suddenly feel jealous of another woman. Especially a woman who's most likely dead. But the sadness in his eyes starts to outweigh my own selfishness.

"I'm sorry. You must really miss her," I say with complete sincerity.

"The pain is unbearable most days." He takes my hand. "But you have managed to divert my attention. You have shown me a way to escape my daily torment and that is why I summoned you and cannot allow further interruptions."

"Interruptions? I don't understand," I admit.

"When you are here I have more control," he says, then looks at me like I should know.

"Wait, what do you mean, you can't allow further interruptions? Are you talking about when I dream?" I ask, knowing I've raised my voice more than I intended.

He lets go of my hand and starts pacing again and I know I've touched a nerve.

"Tell me about your mother." His eyes begin to glow, as if revealing the intensity of his frustration.

"My mom? Why?" I ask.

Why the hell does he want to know about her?

"She raises her hand to you often. Am I correct?"

"No—wait, how do you know that?"

"As I have said, you have a lot to learn."

"Stop with the cryptic talk. Tell me how you know about my mother," I bite out, shoving the covers off my legs.

That gets his attention and he stops in his tracks as his eyes sear into mine. "Be careful, Candice. I do not like your tone," he barks back.

"Answer my question." I pause, knowing I need to cool it with the attitude. "Please?" I ask submissively, hoping if I back off nicely, it will work in him like it usually does on my mother.

Something else I've been well trained for.

"I learn everything about you when you dream. I have seen your mother..." he pauses, "hurt you." He stops again, as if he's physically in pain. "I also know about Brad Davis."

My eyes feel like they're popping out of their sockets because what the fuck?

"Wait a second. Brad?" Unexpectedly, I feel extremely protective of him.

"He likes you very much."

He needs to tell me something I don't know. "Yeah. So..."

"Do you know he followed you here today?"

"Here? To this house?"

"Yes. He even waited for a period of time until I made sure he left," he explains.

"Wait, what did you do?"

"You do not need to concern yourself. I merely gave him a little push to leave."

"Atticus...you can't just go around controlling people like that. Why the hell do you care what he does?"

"Watch your language."

"Answer my question!" I shout.

"Because you are MINE!" His words boom around the room as my palms automatically slam over my ears.

I toss the covers all the way back and sit on the side of the bed, hoping it will snap me out of this nightmare. I need to wake up. I need to stop this craziness.

"You are not leaving, I will not allow it! We are not finished!" he growls.

"Oh, so now I'm your prisoner?" My anger overrides the fact that I should probably be scared shitless right now. I know what he's capable of.

"Do not make me force you to stay," he says in a much calmer voice.

Do I have a choice?" I snap back.

"You always have a choice. The question is, will you make the right one."

"What the hell is that supposed to mean?"

"How do you feel about your mother?" he shoots back.

Stay calm, Candice.

I shrug. "She's an angry alcoholic who has deep issues with abandonment. Is that what you want to hear?"

"I only want the truth."

"Well, that's the sad truth. But she wasn't always like this. We used to be closer but..." I stop, wondering why I'm babbling about her.

"Go on," he encourages me.

"Why do you want to know?" I ask, somehow dreading his answer.

"I can make her go away. Would you like that?" His lips curl into a smile as if he expects this to make me happy.

"Wait...what? Make her go away? What are you talking about?"

"Would you like her out of your life?"

"Uh, no." I can hear my disbelief before it leaves my mouth.

"I do not understand. She has been hurting you for a long time. I think she should pay for her actions."

"She's messed up but that doesn't mean I want her gone."

"Why not? Do you think she will suddenly stop drinking and get her life in order?"

This is insane. He can't play with people's lives like this. I need to do something, anything to wake up from this nightmare!

"Well, no. But, I'll be graduating soon and getting my own pla—"

"Your place is here. With me," he says, fading out of sight.

I wake up screaming on a floor, but this time, I can move more freely. I know exactly where I am because this is reality. This is what the house looks like now. It's no longer candlelit and breathtaking. Atticus is a ghost, he's not real.

The room is almost pitch black save for the light coming from underneath the door. I still have to rely on my sense of touch to find the nearest wall. I don't have time to panic because I'm waving my hands in the air, hoping I don't trip over something. When I touch what feels like the frame of the door, my hands scan anxiously for the knob. Once it's open, I can see a little better through the dim light of the stained glass window. I cautiously peak my head into the hallway and from the looks of it, Atticus isn't here. The entire house is back to being old and abandoned.

My body shakes the whole way down the rickety stairs, winding around extra rooms and hallways until I finally reach the room with the open window. The need to free myself is enough to make me cry. I'm going to run like hell to get home and when I do, I'm going to check on Mom and call Brad. Tears well up in my eyes just thinking about hearing his voice. I keep telling myself this isn't real. All of this is impossible. It has to be even though I feel a strong connection to this house and to Atticus. I can't explain why and couldn't if I tried. It makes my brain hurt just thinking about it.

I'm just about to walk my way to freedom when for some reason, my legs won't go any further.

What the hell?

A powerful dose of euphoria steals my breath, completely taking over my body and my mind. My racing thoughts dissolve. My legs immediately give out and I have to catch myself before falling to the floor. I know this time is different and spectacular and so much more. Nothing matters but Atticus. I feel so incredibly at peace because I can actually feel his soul inside me, as if he's touching every inch of me. I can feel his thoughts and see his memories. For so many years he's been alone and now, I understand. I will never leave him again.

CHAPTER TWENTY-ONE
~~BRAD~~

I'VE BEEN BANGING on Candice's door for the past ten minutes my knuckles are starting to bleed. I'm not even trying to be subtle about it and I'm pretty sure if her neighbors are watching, they think I'm some kind of obsessed boyfriend. I've checked her apartment twice already, hoping she would finally open the door. I don't want to believe it was really her running up to the Emory house but now, I'm questioning everything. What made her crazy and why would she run to that house?

I barely give myself time to process my next thought before sprinting back to my car. Digging for my keys, a rush of adrenaline surges through my body, making me slightly dizzy. The thought of going to the Emory house is starting to mess with my head. I know the rumors aren't true, but it doesn't make it any easier to go back. But no matter what, something wasn't right with Candice, something made her nuts in class. She had a look in her eyes that I haven't seen before on anyone. It was as if she was a completely different person and couldn't concentrate.

I have to go back.

Thankfully, nothing in this town is very far from anything else, so the drive will be short. I've already wasted enough time looking in the wrong places. I just hope I'm right about this because it's the fucking last place I want to be.

Only minutes later, the house comes into full view but I don't see anything out of the ordinary. It looks exactly the same as it did when I was parked outside, staring at it a couple hours ago. I actually think I was expecting it to look different somehow if she were there. I throw the stick into park and cut the engine. There's a clear path from the street to the house so I follow it, racing up to the window. It feels like I'm trespassing, which I am, but I seriously couldn't care less at this point.

The second I step through the window, I scream her name. "Candice!"

I open and close door after door, practically flying from room to room. I wait a few seconds before shouting for her again, hoping like hell she's here.

"Brad?" I hear a faint female voice call out.

Candice.

My head whips immediately toward the sound of her voice. It's coming from upstairs so I race up, taking two steps at a time, hoping I'm going in the right direction, but I don't see her anywhere.

"Candice? Where are you?" I shout, darting my eyes wildly to every possible place she could be. "Can you hear me?"

"Here…"

Her voice is between a whisper and a moan; it scares the shit out of me. I take off in a sprint toward a closed door, pausing only long enough to turn the knob. Total darkness greets me and I feel my gut churning with a thousand tiny needles.

"Where are you? Candice? I can't see anything."

Silence.

There's a lighter in my pocket, the one I keep as a reminder to never smoke cigarettes again. Not after losing my grandfather to lung cancer. I flick the tab on top and watch as sparks dart out, popping up a flame. Squinting my eyes to adjust to the light, I finally see her, standing shakily on a chair. There's something wrapped around her neck. Her neck!

Holy fuck!

I sprint over to her, relieved to see the pretty face of the girl I kissed like I've never kissed anyone before.

"Stop," she whispers, but her eyes are wide and I know she's beyond scared.

It only takes me a second to focus back on the rope. My fingers are trembling because if I make one wrong move, she could fall. The noose is fairly loose and as I extend my arm, I follow the rope and realize it's attached to something on the ceiling.

"What the fuck are you doing?!" I shout, trying to get the rope off her neck.

"Stop, or I'll jump!" she screams.

Her eyes are different. It's as if Candice has left and someone else is talking. My hands suddenly have a mind of their own because they rise and freeze in place.

"Just go," she says, and now I can tell it's her again.

"What is happening to you?" I shout, trying like hell not to let my shaking body throw us both off the chair.

Out of nowhere, a rush of cold air swirls around me and I duck, thinking there might be something flying around my head. I know it's something completely different when the hair on the back of my neck begins to stand up. I'm pretty sure my thumb is burning from the lighter but I barely notice.

"Brad, you have to go. Now!" Candice screams. "Run!"

Before I can respond, I'm slammed against the wall. What feels like a cold hand presses hard around my neck, but I can't see anything.

"Atticus, no!"

A second later, something inside me fills with rage and I'm able to thrust away whatever knocked me back and make a run for Candice. The lighter fell out of my hand and I can't see a damn thing. I wave my arms around, trying to find the chair she's standing on. I'm able to find it a second later and step up on the chair, slipping my arms underneath her as I lift her up. I manage to loosen up the rope enough to lift it around her head. Thankfully, the knot falls apart almost instantly.

"I'm getting you out of here," I say, one arm holding her back and the other beneath her knees, cradling her as I rush us to the door.

Daylight is coming in through a stained glass window and I can see her more clearly. Her face is wet with tears or maybe sweat, I can't be sure. She doesn't look like she's hurt at least.

"I can't leave! You don't understand!" she shouts, struggling to get down.

I keep going, holding on tighter every time she tries to wiggle her way out of my arms. I finally put her down, grabbing her wrist like we're handcuffed, and pull her along with me until I can tell I'm walking on grass.

I double over, panting and trying to keep ahold of her wrist even as she's pulling in the opposite direction. "You're not going back in there."

Suddenly, she stops trying to pull away and stands still for a second, blinking her eyes as if coming out of some kind of trance. "Are you really here?" she asks. "Am I dreaming?"

"Wait, what? You almost tried to kill yourself! What the hell, Candice?" I have to stop myself from shaking the shit out of her because she could have died.

The frightened and confused look on her face begins chipping away at my frustration. I don't have a clue what just happened in that house, but I know I need to get her as far away from it as possible. Then I can ask questions.

"I'm taking you home," I tell her, hoping she doesn't fight me like before. It wouldn't matter if she did because I'd carry her over my shoulder if I had to. Lucky for her, she doesn't and I take her hand to lead her down the path to my car. As soon as she's strapped in, I shut her door, pausing when something about the house catches my attention. My eyes must be playing tricks on me because I think I see a dark figure in an upstairs window. I know for a fact there's no one inside. Jesus, maybe my head hit the wall a little too hard? I pull my eyes away long enough to open my door, and when I glance back up to the window, whatever it was is gone.

CHAPTER TWENTY-TWO

~~BRAD~~

C ANDICE IS STILL a little out of it or in shock, I'm not sure which, when we get to her place. We climb the stairs to her apartment in total silence. I don't even ask if I can come in because she doesn't have a choice, I'm staying with her. God knows what she might do if I leave. What if she goes back to that crazy house? What if she tries to kill herself again? The thought makes me almost nauseated.

I keep a close eye on her as she blindly walks over to the answering machine, like it's always the first thing she does, and hits the flashing red button. She bristles at the sound of the voice.

"Candice? This is Mrs. Stephens, the counselor at Parkview High. Um, honey, I have some bad news. Your mother has been in a car accident and is at Alliance Memorial Hospital. I'm already here and hope you get this soon."

Candice looks like she's just been punched in the gut. I reach out to offer a hug or whatever someone does when they get this kind of news.

"C'mon, I'll take you right now." I grab her hand but she's not moving.

She turns, her unblinking eyes locked with mine. "It was Atticus," she whispers. "He did this."

"I'm sorry. What?" I let go, walking to the kitchen to search for a glass. Clearly, she needs water and maybe something else. "Where's your aspirin?"

She pulls my arm, turning me to face her again. "He did it. He told me he could get rid of her!"

She can't be serious.

"It was him—I know it."

"Wait a second. Are you actually talking about the guy who died in the Emory house?"

"Yes." She pauses, taking my hands. "Atticus. He's real, Brad. I saw him." Her voice is so full of conviction; she's so calm it's a little creepy. "I talked to him."

Holy shit, she actually believes this.

"Candice, there's no way a ghost caused your mother's accident," I snap. "He's not real." I start walking toward the door. "We have to go!"

"You felt him, didn't you? When he pushed you away from me?" Her hands release mine, waving as if to accentuate the truth, but I can't give in to this nonsense.

"You don't know what you're saying." I try to calm her, rubbing her arms up and down. "You were totally out of it. Hell, I'm not entirely convinced your head is with me now. Besides, the room was so dark, I think I just tripped on something."

I'm lying. She knows it, too. I didn't trip on anything, but there's no fucking way a ghost pushed me.

I can see a shift in her expression, consideration taking over the confusion from earlier. Her head moves side to side, her eyes narrowing, like she's playing back every interaction in her head, contemplating her own sanity.

When her eyes drop away from mine I know my words have hurt her. So I take her in my arms and kiss her cheek. "Now, c'mon, we have to get you to your mom. We can talk about this later."

CHAPTER TWENTY-THREE

~~CANDICE~~

B RAD PULLS UP to the front of the hospital and I get out and walk toward the double doors. He was right, I am still a little out of it. Everything feels like it's going in slow motion. Or maybe it's me, I can't tell anymore. I hate that he's been dragged into my mess of a life. I feel like I'm seriously losing my mind. A ghost, who can control me inside and outside of my dreams, apparently drove me to attempt suicide. I was stopped by a guy I met at school, a guy I've kissed twice and am already starting to have feelings for. And now my mother has been in an accident. It's as if I've been living an unconscious existence for the past twenty-four hours, holding on to a truth I no longer understand. Ghosts are real. Ghosts can hurt you.

I'm not sure I can to do this by myself so I just stand here, staring through the glass of the door until I hear footsteps approaching. I don't have to look back; I know they're Brad's. His cadence is easy to detect—strong, yet confident, even now. If it weren't for him, I might be dead and now he's somehow holding the leftover pieces of me together. I've never been so grateful for anyone in my life.

"C'mon." He takes my hand and I practically sigh in relief, glad he's taken the lead. I think he knows I'm not able to do this on my own.

The moment we step through, a rush of disinfectant air swirls around us and I'm suddenly scared of what lies ahead as we make our way toward a woman sitting behind the receptionist's desk.

Brad lets go of my hand and touches the small of my back. "Hi, can you tell us the room number for..." Brad pauses, turning his eyes to me.

"Oh, um, Daisee Crawford," I answer.

The woman smiles back. "Of course. Let me check."

After a few more seconds her expression changes and the smile that was just on her face falls slightly.

"She's in ICU, honey. Family members only."

"I'm her daughter," I quickly reply.

She nods with a troubled smile. "Room 402."

"Thanks." I try to smile back but fail as I reach for Brad's hand. He's the only person in this world I can count on.

The elevator takes forever and the fact that I'm a little claustrophobic doesn't help. Brad must have picked up on my nervousness and pulls me close. "Almost there," he says, and the grappling hooks in my stomach begin to slightly fade.

Finally, the doors open and we're greeted by the smell of rubbing alcohol and an eerily quiet floor.

Brad points to a small lounge area and gives me a squeeze. "I'll wait for you over here."

I nod, not wanting to part with him yet. Holding his hand is the only thing keeping me sane. As soon as he lets go, it physically hurts, like I've lost a limb. I stand frozen as I watch him take a seat, memorizing his exact location. As if that knowledge can help me in some way.

It's up to me now. I need to be that strong girl I've had to be so many times before.

The nurse behind the desk is on the phone. I shift uncomfortably from foot to foot while I wait for her, suddenly distracted when I see a familiar face.

"Mrs. Stephens?" I ask, before I know for sure it's her.

Turning her head, she smiles as our eyes meet. "Oh, thank goodness you're here!"

She comes in for a hug and I automatically hug her back but I can tell something isn't right. "Which one's her room? I ask, looking down the hallway.

"I'll take you to her, but you should probably talk to her doctor first, honey." Her voice quivers like she's nervous and I can't help being startled by her words.

I only realize I'm chewing on my lip when the coppery taste of blood hits my tongue. Mrs. Stephens whispers something to the lady behind the desk then walks back over to me.

"He shouldn't be long, honey," she says, reaching her arm around my shoulder. It feels like she's already consoling me.

What the hell is going on?

"Miss Crawford?" I hear a man's voice call from behind.

I turn around to see a tall, gray-haired older gentleman. "Yes?"

"I'm Dr. Calloway. I've been treating your mother."

"How is she? Can I see her?"

"Yes, but I must warn you, she has sustained a pretty invasive head injury. She's in a coma."

"Is she going to be okay?"

He looks down, as if trying to find the right words. "The first twenty-four hours are the most critical. If she survives through the night, we'll assess her brain activity in the morning. For now she's comfortable."

Warm tears land on my hand and I wipe them away, hoping I don't lose my shit right here, right now. "Can I see her?" I ask as more tears stream down my cheeks.

"Yes, follow me."

I glance over at Mrs. Stephens, who looks like she's about to cry. She gives me a nod, encouraging me to go without her.

And that's it. I'm on my own. No more safely nets.

It's so quiet I can hear our shoes hitting the tile floor with each step. Even the nurses are whispering to each other. It's creepy and feels like I'm crossing into another dimension between here and death.

Dr. Calloway stops just in front of a closed door. The room is almost entirely glass but he's blocking my view.

"Don't let what you see shock you. I promise, your mother isn't in any pain."

When he moves away and I see her and my hand goes directly to my mouth.

Her entire head has been wrapped, only revealing her eyes, nose, and mouth, while tubes are taped to almost every part of her body. The steady pings and beeps from a collection of monitors nearly drown out what the doctor says to me next.

"Only thirty minute visits for now."

I nod as he walks out, reaching for the chair next to her bed. I gently pull it back and take a seat. I stay still for a while, taking it all in, but know in my gut why she's here. Atticus. He's the one who caused this. And even though I can barely stand her, he took her away so I won't hesitate the next time. If she's gone, he must think I'll gladly take my own life. He doesn't know me at all; he's only seen my torment and my fears—all the bad things in my life and none of the good. It's all becoming crystal clear.

"Mom? Can you hear me?" I whisper, taking her hand. It's warm but lifeless and the second I hold it I can tell. There's no hope. She's already gone. She might've been mean as a snake most days, but what am I supposed to do without her? It's clear to me now that I never stopped loving her, I just hated what she was becoming.

I'm starting to go numb, like my mind is switching to autopilot. Things are getting muffled, colors and sounds muted. I've felt like this before. When my Dad left for the last time, I stayed in my room for two days. I didn't eat, hardly slept. I'm pretty sure I was punishing myself because I couldn't punish him.

I bolt out of my chair, tearing into a dead run down the hallway, only stopping once I see Brad. He looks up at me with a look of confusion, but it doesn't matter. The second he stands, I rush into his arms, crashing my head into his chest. He holds me close, squeezing me gently. I look up into his safe brown eyes.

"I h-have to get outta here," I say, gasping for air as Brad's eyes shift past me.

"Candice?"

I don't bother acknowledging her. I can already hear Mrs. Stephens walking toward us.

"I need to speak with you." Her tone sounds as if she already knows I want to run as far away from here as I can.

"It's important," she adds.

I'm so overwhelmed right now I wish my body would just let me pass out so I could skip this part. But I know it won't. I'm just going to be numb.

Autopilot.

"Can we talk in private?"

I don't think I can part with Brad again. In fact, I know I can't. He's the only shred of security I have left. If he were a blanket, I'd wrap myself so tightly in him and never leave.

I turn to Mrs. Stephens. "He gets to come, too," I whisper, reaching for his hand

Brad must feel my anxiety because he pulls me into a sideways hug. We follow the counselor into the chapel across from the ICU doors. No one's here and I'm suddenly grateful for the soothing candlelight illuminating the altar.

Brad and I sit side by side on one end of a pew while Mrs. Stephens sits directly in front, turning around to face us.

She clears her throat, as if contemplating how to tell me something. I already know what she's going to say and want to save her the trouble. I'm fully aware that the doctors have little hope for my mother.

"First of all, I'm so very sorry about your mother." She pauses and I can see the genuine sympathy in her eyes. "But that's not why I brought you in here."

How does she keep doing that?

"I'm going to tell you something that you might not believe." She stops and looks directly at me then takes a deep breath.

"I'm a psychic."

What. The. Hell?

"Wait, what did you say?" I don't disguise my disbelief.

She looks down, turning the ring on her finger a few times before continuing. "Does the name Atticus mean anything to you?"

CHAPTER TWENTY-FOUR

I'M LOOKING AT her but can no longer speak. I see her, but I have nothing to say. My body is shaking like I'm in a sub-zero freezer without anything to keep me warm. Brad immediately squeezes my hand, rubbing his thumb gently over my fingers. The warmth from his hand feels good and I scoot closer.

He puts his arm around me, stroking my arm like he's protecting me, and says, "C'mon, anyone who's lived in this town for even a little while knows about the Emory house."

Mrs. Stephens takes her eyes off me and looks at Brad. "Listen, I don't talk about my abilities to many people, but you have to believe me." Then she locks eyes with me again and says, "You're in danger, honey."

Brad looks down at me then back at Mrs. Stephens. "Are you seriously saying that house is haunted?" His tone drips with disbelief.

"I'm saying that the visions I see are becoming volatile. And yes, the more time she spends there—with him—the more likely something tragic will happen."

I can tell by the look on her face she's not sure either of us believes her. She shakes her head as if frustrated and says, "I know you feel inexplicably drawn to the house, Candice. To him. I know he showed himself to you. I know he makes you dream and comes to you in those dreams.

There's no way this can be happening.

Suddenly finding my voice, I perk up and lean forward, as if getting closer to her will keep all this insanity a secret. "What do you mean by tragic?"

Mrs. Stephens cocks her head, pinching the bridge of her nose with her fingertips. "I saw you standing on a chair, Candice. I also saw Brad being knocked away from you and it was all I could do not to run to that house. But I didn't." She hesitates for a second. "I didn't because then I saw Brad breaking away from him and getting you the hell out of there."

Holy shit.

Mrs. Stephens looks over at Brad, then back to me. "Ten minutes later, as I was about to leave school, I got a call from the police about your mom."

"How the hell—" Brad whispers, his voice trailing off like he just ran out of words.

"Candice," she looks at me dead on, "there is a soul connection between you and Atticus." She starts rubbing her fingers, watching them closely, like they're giving her information. "You knew each other in a past life."

I look up at her, dumbstruck. Whatever I had been expecting, it wasn't this. Staring absently at the candle-light, Mrs. Stephens continues, like she's channeling her thoughts into words.

"I'm pretty sure you and Atticus were lovers."

"This is unbelievable." I look up at Brad, wishing he could make everything go away.

He slips his arm around my shoulder and I nestle back against him. He's probably the only thing keeping me from crumbling into a pile of ash. Then he looks at Mrs. Stephens and says, "Do you realize how crazy this sounds? I mean, I don't get how you know all this, but there's no way that place is haunt—"

"You don't have to believe me, Brad," Mrs. Stephens cuts him off, "but Candice does." She takes a deep breath then lets it out. "Now, does anything seem familiar about the house? Anything at all?"

I glance back up at Brad and he looks a little pissed, but he nods back at me, encouraging me to give in to her shenanigans. So I decide to tell her what I know.

"Maybe. I mean, there were a few times when I thought the house looked familiar. But I was dreaming. That doesn't count, does it?"

"Of course it does. Dreams can sometimes be more real than our own reality." One brow goes up and she cocks her head. "Go on. Tell me everything."

"Well, the house looked completely different in my dream. Like I was seeing it back when it was in its prime. When it was their family home, I guess. That's when I felt like I had been there before."

"Your instincts were right because you have been there before."

"But wait, I'm still confused. How is this possible?" I ask. I'm having a hard time wrapping my brain around this.

Mrs. Stephens shifts in her seat, as if getting ready to tell me all her secrets. "It's kind of hard to explain, actually, but I can try." She pauses, choosing her words carefully. "Remember your first day of school?"

I nod, saying nothing because I don't want her to stop.

"Well, I could sense something from you right away. Mostly that you were a troubled girl, which consequently, made you more open to my abilities."

"So, you already knew I was..." I pause, searching for her word, "troubled?"

"Yes. You see, I'm not only psychic, I can also pick up on certain emotions and they in turn, help me read you."

"Isn't everyone nervous on their first day of school?" I ask, hoping I don't offend her.

"Sure, but you were different. You gave off a certain vibe that I picked up on immediately."

Mrs. Stephens looks at Brad, then back to me. "I know about the bruises on your wrists, honey." She pauses, as if giving herself permission to say more. "And your cheek."

Brad pulls me away from the warm spot I was nestled in and for the first time I see rage in his eyes. "That son-of-a-bitch hurt you?"

"No." I glare at Mrs. Stephens; I can tell she knows. And I'm pretty sure she's aware Brad has no idea about my mother. "It's not like that."

Brad takes both of my hands and inspects my wrists, but the bruises are barely visible. Almost gone. Then he looks up to my face, gently gliding the back of his palm along my cheek. "Who hurt you?"

"I-I never wanted you to know. I..." I stop because I'm about to cry.

"Never wanted me to know what?" he whispers.

"When my mother drinks, she sometimes loses her temper." A single tear drops from my cheek and lands on his thumb.

"Jesus, Candice," he says, pulling me back into him and wrapping both arms around me.

Mrs. Stephens pulls a tissue out of her purse and hands it to me. I wipe my eyes and instantly feel relieved that Brad knows about Mom's drinking and her awful temper. I've never trusted anyone to know this much about my life but I can trust him. It feels like an enormous weight has been lifted from this burden I've tried to hide for years.

Out of the blue something hits me and my eyes dart back to Mrs. Stephens. "Oh my God, the picture!" I blurt out.

"What picture?" Brad and Mrs. Stephens say at the exact same time. If the situation weren't so serious, it would have been funny.

"I found a picture in my mother's room, on her nightstand. An old picture of the Emory house. At the time it kind of freaked me out, and I meant to ask Mom about it. She was never in a good enough mood. I totally forgot about it until now."

"Oh, no." Mrs. Stephens closes her eyes for a second then focuses directly at me. "He must have put it there—somehow."

"What? How?" I ask, tilting my head.

"I don't know what the picture symbolizes, but Atticus is definitely capable of much more than I thought," she says, talking more to herself than to us.

"What do you mean?" I ask, swallowing back the knot forming in my throat.

"It means…." She stops then says, "Wait, your mom. Has she always had an addiction problem?"

Wondering why she's going there, I answer, "Well, no. I mean, she's always smoked, but her drinking, and her temper seem to be getting worse. I figured it was from all the stress she puts herself through. Why?"

"I think he might be feeding off her, too." Mrs. Stephens looks at us and shakes her head, as if knowing she's putting the puzzle pieces together too quickly for us to keep up. "Addiction is one of the easiest forms of energy they can consume."

"So you're telling me that a freaking ghost is what's making Mom's addiction get worse?" I ask, hoping I'm wrong.

"Without a doubt. If her drinking and the violence, even her anger, are getting worse, especially since you moved here, they're most likely all a direct result of his power over her."

"But she's never even been to that house."

"Doesn't matter. He's connected to you and through you he can get to her."

"The accident." I whisper, looking up at Mrs. Stephens. "He did it. He said he could get rid of her."

"Dear God." Her hand instantly goes to her forehead, then down and finally shoulder-to-shoulder.

"Did you not see that?" I ask, trying to stop my body from trembling.

Mrs. Stephens shifts in her seat. "No. No, I didn't." She pauses. "I'm guessing because my connection is only with you."

Brad tightens his grip around my back as he continues to glare at Mrs. Stephens. "Can he really do that? Does he have that kind of power?"

She looks down and shakes her head. "I—I..." She stops as if a thousand thoughts are running through her head. "Yes, apparently he does." Her concerned eyes shift to me. "The timing makes sense."

"Jesus." Brad turns away for a second then he glances up at Mrs. Stephens. "But it still doesn't answer the question of how the picture got in her mother's room."

"He did it through teleportation." She answers with more confidence this time then goes on to explain, thank goodness. "Teleporting is when a spirit can actually move an object from one place to another. It's one of the hardest things they can master, but clearly, he managed to do that as well."

She picks up her purse like she's just remembered something and places it on her lap. One hand holds it open and the other bobs back and forth inside, searching for something.

"Here, you're going to need this." She hands me a bag filled with some kind of dark powder. I take it, hoping she'll explain. "It'll keep you safe, but not for long." She looks at Brad, then back at me, as if telling us both will ensure proper use. "This is black salt and you must sprinkle it in each corner of your bedroom and again around the corners of your bed. It will keep Atticus from being able to attack you physically. The good thing is, you don't have to use a lot for it to work."

"Wait, if all this is actually true, I thought you said he could only teleport things. How can he attack Candice?" Brad asks with renewed assertiveness.

"He's actually been attacking Candice for a while now." She pauses and meets my eyes, nodding. "In her dreams."

I look up because she's right. "You know about that, too?"

She dismisses my question and keeps talking. "Right now, it's important that you listen carefully because this isn't going to stop. Atticus is connected to you through your past life and when you died, he took his life because of it."

Brad perks up. "Hold on a minute. This past life nonsense, how do you know about that?"

Mrs. Stephens raises her brows and nods, as if he just reminded her to explain that part. "You know how I told you I could see what was happening even when I'm not there?"

"Yeah," Brad says, cocking his head.

"Well, there's also tons of residual energy in that house, too."

"Okay, but what does that mean?" he asks.

"It means the walls, the wood, every fiber of that house has soaked up the past. Sort of like a sponge." She looks back and forth to both of us then keeps going. "And when I say past, I mean mostly tragic things that have happened. Like when Atticus hung himself."

"So," Brad chimes in, "are you saying you can see that, too?"

"Yes." She pauses. "Well, sort of. I can see flashes of images and feel the emotions that go along with them. Especially if they're catastrophic. And if you've been doing this as long as me, you start getting good at deciphering the pieces of a story."

"Okay," Brad says, "So, you think Candice used to be the girl Atticus killed himself over?"

"Without a doubt," Mrs. Stephens says. "Her name was Josephine."

Brad glances over to me and I nod, then his eyes are back to Mrs. Stephens. "But where does Josephine tie into all of this?"

"I thought you'd never ask." She smiles and looks at me. "Candice, you were my clue. When I met you on that first day and handed you your schedule, our fingers touched and I saw images of you as someone else. Someone from the past. That's never happened to me before." She rubs her fingers again and continues.

"As time went by and I realized you had a connection to the house, I figured maybe it went deeper. Quite frankly, it was driving me nuts that I couldn't piece together you and the other woman I saw in you. So, I did a little research at the library and I was right. I found some old newspaper pictures from right around the time Lilburn was established in 1890. Actually, it was still McDaniel until 1910, when it was officially named Lilburn. There was one photo in particular that caught my eye. It was a picture of Atticus standing next to the woman I saw in you. I couldn't believe it at first and ended up staring at it for a couple of minutes. But it all came together for me and I was one hundred percent certain, you were her in a past life.

Brad shifts in his seat and jerks his head to me. "Hang on a second, didn't you say the picture you found had that date on it?"

"Holy crap, yes!" I exclaim, my hands shaking. "It said 1910."

We both look up at Mrs. Stephens, who already appears to have the answer to our next question.

"1910 was the year the Emory family tried to sell their house. It's a real estate picture, if you will."

"Why would he put that picture on Candice's mom's nightstand?" Brad asks.

Mrs. Stephens has a faraway look in her eyes. "I'm not entirely sure, but my guess is he was sending a message. He'll never allow it to be sold. He doesn't plan on leaving; it's his house. And to my knowledge, every time someone tries to sell the house, it always falls through."

"Who owns it now?" I ask.

"Property records show it's still owned by the Emory family."

My mind is racing over a thousand different things; this makes a thousand and one. And how is it possible that even if I were reincarnated, I have zero recollection of it?

"One more thing." I look up at Mrs. Stephens. "Help me understand that if I was Josephine, then why can't I remember her?" My head hasn't stopped spinning. I'm not sure I can take much more of this.

She's about to say something, then pauses like she needs to word it properly. "I believe we all live past lives and ninety-nine percent of us don't remember any of them. There are a select few who do, but like I said, most of us are oblivious." She takes a deep breath. "Josephine died of tuberculosis and it was fairly sudden. Atticus pretty much lost his mind over it. Clearly, he gave no thought to what he was about to do. He simply reacted."

"So that's why Atticus killed himself," I say, not expecting confirmation.

"Yes." Mrs. Stephens looks me in the eye. "He hung himself from the second story balcony."

My stomach tightens as the nausea swirls around in my stomach. I see Brad close his eyes. And just then, at that exact moment, it's like we both just figure out why I was standing on that chair with a noose around my neck. Likely it was almost identical to the way Atticus did it nearly a hundred years before.

Brad turns to me and whispers, "I won't let him hurt you. Even if you were Josephine once, you're Candice now."

Mrs. Stephens places her hand on Brad's knee. "You need to keep her away from that house because I'm pretty sure Atticus wants a companion. Someone who will take their own life and be damned like him." She shifts in her seat. "The black salt will help with protection, but it's only temporary. It isn't strong enough to work for very long, so keep using it. He'll get into your head again because he's attached himself to you and can control you, but this time, you'll be ready."

Mrs. Stephens has more confidence than I have at this moment, though her pep talk was encouraging. It feels like there's a hurricane brewing inside my body, waiting to destroy everything in its path. I'm scared, I'm angry, and I want to run far away and forget ever moving to this fucking town.

My body is starting to tremble again and I feel Brad tighten his arms around me. It helps, even feels good, but I'm legitimately losing it. As much as I can usually fake my way through everything, I can't today. Today is the day I will have to give control to someone else.

I bury my face in Brad's chest, not realizing I'm sobbing like a little kid until I hear his voice.

"I need to get her out of here," he whispers.

"Yes, I think that's a good idea," Mrs. Stephens says, placing her hand on my shoulder. "She needs to rest to gather some strength, but don't let her out of your sight."

Brad stands up, pulling me with him as we turn and walk out of the chapel. I wipe tears on his shirt, looking up to see the muscle in his jaw twitch several times. The concerned look on his face stabs at my heart. He's a good guy. I just met him. He shouldn't have to be this strong. Especially not in this dark and twisted world I've now involved him in. I've got to pull myself together somehow. It's me Atticus wants, not him.

"Where are we going?" I ask softly as we make our way to the parking lot.

His jaw twitches again. "My house," he says flatly, opening my door. "We'll come back to check on your mom in a few hours."

I turn around and meet his eyes. "You believe her, don't you?"

Brad shuts his eyes for a moment and I can tell he's wrestling with himself with what to say. Then, he surprises me and nods slightly.

Suddenly, I want to kiss him. The fact that he believes her, me, any of this lunacy reverses my mood and I feel like I can breathe again. Funny what a burst of validation can do.

Standing on the tip of my toes, I place my hands on either side of his face while tears stream down mine. "You know the feeling you get when you finally have a glimmer of hope?" I smile, looking down at his beautiful mouth. "You just gave that to me."

Brad's arm reaches around my shoulder, moving my body closer to his. I pull in a breath as he gently kisses me with his soft, warm lips. A wave of lust surges between my legs as I wrap my arms tightly around his neck. He's intoxicating and before I know it, we're practically devouring each other, allowing this one, amazing kiss to take away all the stress of the past few hours. With every tease of his tongue I want him more.

Brad must be sensing it and pulls away. "We should go," he whispers, taking my hand as we walk to his car. "But I need to tell you something."

I look up and can almost feel the sadness in his eyes. "Yeah?" I say, hoping I didn't push him too far. I feel like I'm acting like a complete slutty bipolar lunatic.

His palm slides down the side of my face, bringing my eyes to his as if he wants me to really hear him, and says, "Ending that kiss was probably the hardest thing I've ever had to do."

CHAPTER TWENTY-FIVE

B RAD TURNS INTO his driveway, still managing to hold my hand as he shifts into park. It's become something he does and I didn't realize until now how much I liked it. I'm not sure I've ever felt this protected or safe around anyone. I'm also not sure I know what to make of it. How, after all we've been through, can he still want to be anywhere near me? I have nothing to offer him but complete and utter chaos. By now, he has to know that. And in a matter of seconds, I'm going to meet his parents and even stay at his house because he and I both know that inside, I'm crumbling to pieces. He's the only human being I've ever met in my life that I feel like I've known far longer than I actually have.

"Wait." I touch his arm. "What are you going to tell your parents?"

"I'll just tell them the truth," he says, clenching his jaw.

"What? You can't do that," I say, wondering why he thinks that's remotely a good idea.

"Yeah, I can. I'll tell them your mom has been in a bad accident and is in ICU."

A rush of guilt hits me; I almost forgot about my mother, who's lying in a hospital bed in critical condition. Not likely to wake up. My head starts to throb almost immediately.

"But what do we say about why I'm here?" I ask, still in awe he's not running for his life away from me.

He looks at me, cocking his head like it's obvious. "Because I don't want to leave you alone."

～～

I'm exhausted and my headache is getting worse. After Brad and I finish spreading the black salt around the guest room bed, he hands me a couple of Tylenol, insisting I get some sleep. I don't have the strength to argue when he pulls back the blankets.

"C'mon." He smiles and moves aside so I can get in. I take off my shoes and slide in, trying not to sigh when he tucks the blankets around me. He stands by the nightstand with his hands in his pockets, as if struggling with what to say or do next.

"I'm okay," I say, trying to reassure him.

"I hope so. I feel helpless," he admits, stepping up so close to me I almost forget about the pounding in my head. He kisses my lips ever so gently, like I'm made of glass.

"Brad," I whisper, reaching my hand to his, "I don't know what would have happened today if it weren't for you."

He takes it and smiles but I can see the worry behind his eyes. He delicately takes a strand of my hair between his fingers and kisses it gently, as if treasuring every piece of me. I almost lose my breath. I want him. All of him.

He leans back down but this time kisses my cheek. "Get some rest. I'll call the hospital and give them our number."

"Oh yeah, thank you," I say, closing my eyes.

A few minutes later I hear a knock on the door while I'm rubbing my temples, trying to ease the worsening pain.

"Yes?" I say softly.

Brad's face shows through the slightly opened door. "I thought you'd like to know that your mom is the same. Stable but critical." Then he stops, as if seeing me for the first time. "Whoa, are you okay?"

I grunt because talking makes the throbbing worse.

He sits on the side of the bed next to me, reaching for a blanket draped over the edge. "Jesus, it's cold in here."

My eyes are closed but I can feel him tucking the blanket in around me as if I were a little kid. "Thanks," I whisper, "I'm sure the medicine will kick in soon."

"I hope so." He pauses, stroking my arm. "Call me if you need anything."

I don't have to look up to see the worry on his face. It's there, loud and clear, in his voice.

"I'll be back in a little while. Try to sleep," he says then gently closes the door.

~~

I hear footsteps and open my eyes but I know they're not Brad's. I don't know how long I've been asleep, but I feel sick and exhausted at the same time.

"Hello, Candice."

His voice is still so beautiful and I reach out to him. "How did you find me?" I don't know why I asked; I already know the answer. He's part of me now.

"You must come with me." It feels like cool fingers are tapping on my cheek.

When I push up on my elbows and look around, he's not there. I turn to look out the window and see the edge of the sun resting just above the horizon. I've been asleep for a couple of hours.

"Atticus?" I call out, but I he doesn't answer.

Lifting the covers, I step out of bed to get a better look and I'm right, I'm alone. Instantly, my head begins to throb again and I hear his voice. But it's not coming from inside the room; he's in my thoughts.

"If you want the pain to stop, you must return to me." Every time he speaks, the pain eases a bit, then returns with a vengeance—worse than before.

I'm having a hard time trying to think, but I know I have to leave as soon as possible. I rush over to the window, hoping I can sneak out without Brad noticing. I know he wouldn't let me leave and it pricks at my gut to betray him but I have no choice. The pain is too intense and the only way to make it go away is to do what Atticus wants. And what he wants is me.

My hands start to shake and I nearly break every nail trying to get the window open. I squint for a better look at the frame and realize it's locked. I'm so desperate to get out I have to stop myself from kicking in the glass.

You can do this.

Closing my eyes, I rest my head against the glass for a moment, trying to will the pain away. I reach up and manage to turn both locks, then slowly pull the window up. The seal makes a loud screech and I automatically stop, ducking as if doing so will make the sound go away.

Shit.

I try again, only this time, I pull up faster, hoping it won't be as loud. It works and barely makes a sound. I silently thank God because the pain is starting to blur my vision.

Pushing on the screen with my hands, I manage to get it off without too much force. The bushes just below make it hard to climb out without breaking a limb or two but I can't worry about that right now. The only thing that matters is getting to that house because the faster I run, the better my head feels.

Atticus is rewarding me.

CHAPTER TWENTY-SIX

I T'S TOTALLY DARK outside by the time I reach the house, but I know my way around now. The path, the trees...navigating them is becoming second nature to me and I easily make it to the window. Once I get inside, I run to the staircase and pause before going further.

"Atticus, you know I'm here. Where are you?" I shout. As usual, he's silent but I don't expect to still have so much pain.

What is he doing?

I take the stairs two at a time, stopping when a strong breeze whips my hair. He's right behind me. I can feel him. Another gust of wind swirls around my shoulders but this time it's much stronger, pushing my body forward enough that I have to catch myself, tightly gripping the banister.

I feel his breath on my neck as he whispers, "You should never have left me."

"I—I'm sorry," I say, closing my eyes at the fury in his voice.

"You are not sorry!" he roars, appearing directly in front of me.

I don't dare move and hold back the urge to run like hell. We stand, locked at the eyes, and suddenly, I see my mother's eyes instead of his.

"Leave your mother out of this," he demands, slamming his fist against the wall. "She is no longer your concern!"

I flinch, realizing his power is much stronger than he's ever revealed. "How did you know—"

"I know far more than you can imagine, Candice."

"Was it really you?" I ask. My heart feels like it's about to burst through my chest, but I have to know. "Did you cause my mother's accident?"

"Yes," he begins to pace at the top of the stairs, "and as I said, very soon, she will no longer be your daily burden. Nor will your little boyfriend, for that matter." His eyes begin to glow in the darkness. He's proud of himself.

I shut my eyes because I can't look at him anymore without losing concentration. Out of nowhere, he's standing next to me and I'm actually more frightened than I've ever been in my entire life.

"You have to stop, Atticus," I whisper, losing my breath. He's so close I can actually feel his energy. I'm trembling so much my teeth are chattering, but I'm doing everything I can to hold my ground.

My eyes flash open when he laughs and says, "Black salt has no effect on me. The only way you can save your mother or your boyfriend is to submit to me completely."

My body turns ice cold with his words. I automatically think of Brad. Just the thought of him makes me want to fight harder, harder than I've ever fought before. Standing up to him is my only choice.

"What...you want me to hang myself? Like you did?" I bite back with renewed strength because suddenly, I have something more to fight for. "You think you knew me in some kind of ridiculous past life?"

I don't have to look up to know he's enraged. I can feel it like a strong wave of water, pushing me back in its wake.

"Your soul has always belonged to me!" He yanks my arm, pulling me toward the balcony. I feel the railing shake as he pushes me against it, catching a glimpse of the floor below. My head and my heart are still pounding and I'm seriously starting to fear my own mortality.

"You actually think killing me is the answer?" I scream back.

"No, it has to be your choice!" he admits, glaring at me.

"My choice? Why in God's name would I choose that?"

His beautiful eyes soften a little and I almost think he might be struggling with his emotions, afraid to show me too much. He starts to pace again; it must help him focus.

"We are meant together. You promised!" he shouts.

"I have no idea what you're talking about. I never promised you anything!" I shout back.

He stops, looking up at me with glowing eyes. I lose my concentration for a split second, then force my eyes away.

"We promised each other everything, Josephine."

CHAPTER TWENTY-SEVEN
~~BRAD~~

THE BACK DOOR opens and I already know it's Mom. The Family Law office she manages closes at five thirty every day, even though most of the attorneys stick around longer. Sometimes Mom stays after too, picking their brains about class action suits and indictments. Especially if there's a case she's interested in. Even without going to law school, it wouldn't surprise me if she could pass the Bar exam.

"Hey," I call over my shoulder.

"Hi, honey. What are you making?"

"Mac and cheese." I pause because I think I hear Candice. Maybe she's awake?

"How 'bout I make us a couple sandwiches to go with it?" Mom suggests, opening the pantry door.

I better tell Mom what's going on before Candice beats me to it. If she walks out of the guest room looking like she just woke up, it might be a little bit of a shock. The good thing is, Mom prides herself on helping oth-

ers, so there's a pretty decent chance she'll be okay with
it.

"I need to talk to you."

"Sure. What's up?" She sets the bread on the counter
and pats my back.

"I kind of told a friend she could stay with us for a
couple of days."

"Wait a minute, you kinda did what?" Her brows
rise.

"I know, I should have talked to you first, but hear
me out. Her name is Candice, and well, her life is pretty
much a mess right now." I stumble through the words,
hoping Mom doesn't detect how freaked out I really
am.

"What do you mean, a mess?" Mom asks, a look of
concern already showing on her face.

"She just found out this afternoon that her mom
was in a really serious car wreck. The doctors aren't
sure she's gonna make it." The words come out with a
little more ease this time.

"Poor thing...that's awful." She pauses then says,
"I've never heard you talk about her before. How do
you know her?"

She's right, I haven't talked about Candice at all.
But there are a lot of things I don't tell my parents and
right now, they're just gonna have to trust me. Thankfully, I'm talking to Mom about this before Dad gets
home.

Might as well tell her the truth. There's no harm
in it. "I met her at school," I say, grabbing the colander

from the cabinet. "She and her mom just moved here and don't really know anyone."

"Well, I'm not sure your father is going to approve of this," she says as she walks away, grabbing a glass from the cabinet.

"Mom, it would only be for a night or two. She's not staying in my bedroom or anything. I just don't want her to be alone right now...she's pretty upset."

She turns around and smiles, cocking her head. "You like her, don't you?"

Shit.

"Yeah, Mom, I like her," I confess, knowing I'll never hear the end of it.

"Okay," she says, pointing a butter knife in my direction. "But no hanky-panky in the middle of the night."

"Jesus, Mom. I'm pretty sure that'll be the last thing on her mind," I say, pulling the lid off the nearly boiling pot of water.

"Okay, calm down." She pauses, as though realizing I'm pretty worried about her "I'll talk to your father about it when he gets home. Hopefully, he'll understand.

"Thanks, Mom."

She pats my back again. "Where is this girl?"

"Oh, she's sleeping in the guest room. She wasn't feeling well when we got home. But I thought I heard her moving around a few minutes ago."

Before I can say any more, the phone rings, pulling me away from the now boiling pot. I reach for the receiver, hoping it's not bad news.

"Hello?"

"Yes, this is Alliance Hospital. Is this the number for Candice Crawford?" the caller asks.

"Yes, hang for a second and I'll get her." I'm pretty sure she's awake, so I put the receiver on the counter and walk down the hallway. I'm a little surprised there's no light coming from underneath the door and wonder if I was wrong. Maybe she's still sleeping? I hate to wake her, but this might be important.

After giving the door three knocks, I call her name. "Candice…you awake?" I say a little louder than a whisper.

She doesn't answer, so I try again, only this time, I knock harder.

After a few more knocks, I'm met with the same silence, so I turn the knob, gently opening the door. The curtains are blowing in the breeze. My stomach drops as I rush to the bed.

Shit!

She's gone.

My heart feels like it's hammering against my ribs as I rush out of the room, almost tripping over the blanket I'd placed over her only a few hours ago. Yanking my keys off the counter, I catch a glimpse of my mother's confused expression.

"What's wrong?" she asks, her voice filled with urgency.

I try to keep my cool, giving Mom a look like this isn't a big deal. "She's gone. But I think I know where she is." I smile, but inside I'm dying.

I practically fly to my car. Why did I lock the damn door? The extra seconds it takes only amps up my adrenaline, as I will my fingers to stop shaking. I'm barely sitting before starting the engine. My dad is probably going to kill me for leaving skid marks as I tear out of the driveway. My entire body is on overdrive but it's somehow helping me stay focused.

I need a plan.

Reaching in my pocket, I pull out what's left of the black salt Mrs. Stephens gave us, hoping like hell it will help.

Please let her be okay.

It's a short drive, but I hit every fucking red light in town so I start taking short cuts through neighborhoods, breaking God knows how many speed limits on the way.

I slam on the brakes for one last red light, realizing it's damn near a miracle I haven't been pulled over. My hands grip the steering wheel so tightly my knuckles have gone white. I need to calm my shit down and come up with some kind of plan before I do something stupid, but the only thing I think of is sneaking up on the fucker and grabbing Candice before he knows I'm there.

After what feels like an eternity, the light finally turns green and I hit the gas, screeching the tires against the pavement. I shift quickly into second gear, then third, and finally into forth.

Just a few more blocks and I'll cut off my headlights.

I check my pocket again, touching the small lump of black salt. It's my only defense. I have no idea if it will work but I have to do something. I just hope like hell I'm not too late. I'm instantly nauseated just thinking about it.

I make a right on Oak Lawn, parking two houses down before cutting the engine. I sneak out, barely clicking the door shut as I duck and run, sneaking across the lawn like I'm about to rob the place.

The house is quiet but as I get closer and slip through the broken out window, I can hear talking in the distance. I try to be as quiet I can, but my heart is practically bursting through my chest, requiring me to take quick breaths. If I'm not careful, I'm sure they'll hear me coming by that alone. I want so badly to call for her but force myself to stop and listen. A few seconds go by before I hear something. It's faint but it sounds like a male voice coming from upstairs.

Atticus.

Ducking behind the staircase, I close my eyes and stop to concentrate because somehow it helps. I pray I hear her voice. Please be okay. Please be okay.

I look up the second I hear what sounds like a scream.

Candice.

She's still alive.

Thank God.

Bolting up the stairs, I climb faster than I've ever climbed before. I don't care if I'm heard. I don't care if he attacks me. I just want to get to her.

Her voice becomes louder with each step and I can tell now that she's crying. I make my way just to the right of the door and slowly extend my neck to look inside the room. It's completely candlelit. This time I can see everything.

She's back on the chair with the noose around her neck, holding on to the knot above her head. Her eyes are fixed on the wall and she's perfectly still.

"Hello, Brad," he says.

And there he is in full form.

Atticus

He's tall like me, wearing what looks like an old fashioned suit. If I didn't know any better, I'd think he was in costume.

I can barely believe my eyes and shake my head, hoping this isn't real.

"Perhaps I should have taken care of you when I had the chance." His indignant tone hits me square in the face, pulling me out of my disbelief.

"Let her go!" I shout, looking directly into his eyes, ready to pounce.

His eyes actually glow, his cheekbones rising to form a vicious, villainous smile. A pleased smile, like he's just discovered my deepest thoughts. He takes two steps toward me and laughs. It makes my insides shake. When he speaks, his voice is calculated and calm.

"As you can tell, black salt does not work on me."

"I said, let her go!" I shout again, keeping my hand close to my pocket. If he's bluffing, I may have a chance.

Atticus looks up at Candice then back down to me. "If you sincerely love her, you will turn around and leave and I will spare your life. You cannot save her now."

"Fuck you, I'm not going anywhere," I hiss back.

"And it will be your last mistake." He vanishes, his voice still echoing in the room.

Just like that, Atticus is gone.

I don't have time to think about what I just saw or calculate the impossibility of it. I have to get to Candice. The moment I lock eyes with her, a hard jolt to my chest catapults me back, slamming my body against the wall. The pain is sharp, taking my breath away, and before I know it, I'm on the floor, unable to take a deep breath.

"Sorry you stayed?" His voice, filled with demented sarcasm booms around the room.

Atticus is nowhere to be found, but I know he's watching my every move. Reaching for my front pocket, I try like hell to hide that I'm touching the tip of the bag before pulling it out. It hurts to move and I still can't get a deep breath, but I have do something.

Catching movement, I look up as Atticus appears directly in front of me. If I hadn't seen him appear and disappear twice with my own eyes, I'd probably think they were playing tricks on me.

"Let her go," I get out but my voice is weak from lack of air. I glance over at Candice, who's still staring at the wall like some kind of zombie.

He laughs heartily, as if I'm making a joke. "I commend your chivalry—of that you can be sure—however, you are fighting a losing battle." He slowly bends down to my level, his face only inches from mine, smiling like a he has me right where he wants me. I take that as my sign and throw what's left of the black salt in his face.

I've surprised him. His eyes go wide and he suddenly disappears, his cry lingering in the room.

Holy shit, did it work?

I don't have time to wonder, forcing myself to my knees. It hurts like a mother but I need to get to Candice before he comes back. Why isn't she trying to get down on her own? I raise my head and see her still standing there. She's in some sort of trance—just like the last time.

"Candice!" I shout as loudly as I can, but there's still no reaction.

Reaching for the chair for support, I pull myself up, wincing from the pain but manage to stand up when I hear her soft voice.

"Brad, you have to leave," Candice whispers, as if trying to keep it a secret. "Go."

Shit, does she even know she's been catatonic most of the time I've been here?

"I'm not leaving without you, and…" I stumble toward her but catch myself, dazedly thinking of other ways to get her off the chair, since lifting her might be impossible. "Atticus is not only trying to get you to kill yourself, he's also fucking with your head."

"Brad, watch out!" she screams.

Before I can respond, my body is thrust against the wall again. This time I definitely feel a rib crack and the room begins to instantly spin. My legs quickly betray me as I slide down the wall into a sitting position, fighting the urge to throw up. Taking a deep breath is even more impossible and I struggle for sips of air.

After a second or two, the pain eases up and I'm able to pull up my heavy head. I watch as Atticus approaches, prowling toward me like a big, ghostly cat. I struggle to get to my feet, but stumble back, hitting my head hard against the wall. I feel warm blood roll down my neck.

I'm beaten and he knows it.

"You had a chance to leave, yet you chose to stay," he comments, looking genuinely curious. "Do you love her?"

Ignoring him, I attempt to get back up but he stands over me, demanding my answer. I slowly look up at him, trying to keep his attention away from my hand, gathering some of the fallen salt.

"Answer me!" he shouts as animal-like shadows begin crawling along the ceiling.

If I weren't in so much pain, the horrific show above my head would be terrifying, but I'm finally able to get a full breath and force my legs to pull me up. Immediately, my hand tosses the last bits of black salt in his face. He disappears again but this time, I'm ready for it. I know I only have a few seconds to get Candice down.

"Brad, run!" Candice shrieks.

I turn around to see Atticus flying straight toward me, both hands stretched out, aiming directly for my throat.

"Stop...I love him!" Candice cries out.

Atticus whips his head at Candice and I watch her take what looks like a gut punch, pushing her right off the chair.

"No!" I scream as her body catches on the rope. I can't breathe for the agonizing moments it takes for the crappy knot to unravel and her body to crash to the floor.

Atticus is gone and I'm no longer blocked. I slip on the salt grains, struggling to regain my balance as I run to her. The pain isn't even affecting me when I jerk her body to me, taking the pressure off her neck as I pull the rope away. I cradle her in my arms, rocking her back and forth. "C'mon, breathe!"

I gently lay her on the floor, desperately gasping for my own breath. Pressing my lips on hers, I give her three quick blows of what's left of the air in my lungs.

"Please, Candice," I whisper in her ear.

I want to cry when her lids begin to flutter and I instantly kiss her lips, her hair, her face. The rope made a mark on her neck, but I could tell when I pulled it off it wasn't tied well enough to support her weight.

Thank God.

"Holy shit, are you okay?" I whisper, easing her into a sitting position.

She looks up at me and smiles weakly, a single tear rolling down her cheek. "I think so," she says, glancing around the room in confusion. "What happened?"

"We can talk later, we have to go." I scoop her up, ignoring the incredible pain in my ribs, and stand her on her feet. "Are you okay to walk?"

"I'm not sure, my ankle is killing me," she says, looking up at me. When she meets my eyes, her face changes. "Wait, why are you bleeding?" She reaches a hand out to touch me but I bat it away.

"I'm okay," I say, rushing to get her down the stairs. I take her arm and wrap it around my neck, helping her with each step. We lean clumsily on each other, taking one stair at a time. It's hardly my idea of a quick getaway, but a huge sense of relief rushes over me when we finally reach the first floor.

The house is quiet, almost too quiet, and as I glance around, I can actually feel that something isn't right. Ignoring my instincts, I keep going, trying to pick up our pace when the broken window comes into full view.

Candice looks up at me and I immediately know something's wrong. "The pain in my head. It's back... I—it's too much." She cries, holding her head like she's about to pass out.

"Almost there, baby," I whisper, kissing the top of her head. "Just a few more steps."

A sudden burst of ice-cold wind swirls viciously around the room, stopping us in our tracks. Candice instantly grabs my arm, turning me to face her, and I wince in pain.

"It's me he wants, not you!" she shouts, slamming both hands to her head. "Go! Now!"

"I'm not leaving without you!" I yell, pulling her with me. That same weird stare washes over her face again and I yank on her arm, trying to snap her out of it myself. "He's trying to control you! Fight it, Candice!"

Out of nowhere, giant black shadows begin to take shape on every wall. I jerk Candice to my chest as I watch the grotesque creatures scamper in distorted motion, hissing as if communicating with one another. Impossibly, the shadows pull away from the walls as their blacker-than-black, animal-like figures begin surrounding us as, forming a connected circle. The distinct formation of a man appears in the center.

Atticus.

His eyes are now glowing red. "Did you actually think you could escape me?"

Instant nausea hits my gut but I manage to keep hold of Candice. She's looking at Atticus with a blank stare while he glares back like he has her under some kind of horrific spell. She whimpers, tears streaming down her face. I can tell he's hurting her when she fights to get away from me. We're surrounded and I don't have any options except distraction.

"Leave her the fuck alone!" It hurts like hell to scream but somehow, it worked. She's no longer fighting me and I watch as his attention immediately shifts to me. Daggers stab the inside of my skull. I don't even know I've let Candice go until I feel my hands pound against my temples.

"Get away from her! She is mine!" Atticus shouts as Candice starts walking toward him.

I try to reach for her but when I do, the daggers become impossibly worse. Sharper. Stronger. I'm out of choices. It feels like I'm dying.

"Candice!" a voice suddenly shouts from outside the window.

Atticus jerks his head toward the sound, the shadow creatures instantly evaporating into thin air. I fall to my knees, no longer able to keep up with the pain in my head and ribs. A wisp of smoke hits my nose and I look up to see milky clouds filling the room. Immediately the daggers in my head go away but Candice is still staring blankly, frozen in place.

"Brad, grab her hand!" a voice calls to me and I can finally think clearly enough to recognize the voice.

Mrs. Stephens.

She's in the house, holding a stick or maybe a bunch of weeds, I can't tell through the fog of smoke. All I do know is, Atticus is nowhere in sight.

Thank Christ.

I reach up to Candice and take her hand, though it hurts like hell, as Mrs. Stephens begins chanting.

"I banish you from this house. Only love, light, and peace may enter." She blows on the burning stick, making the tip brighter as scattered embers begin to fall.

She glances over at me, then back to Candice, like she's calculating what to do next. She pulls out a vile of something dark and she holds it as if were a newborn baby, taking off the lid with extreme care. The second she pours what looks like black water into her palm, the most horrific screams echo in the room.

"I banish you from this house. Only love, light, and peace may enter," she shouts again. Her eyes scan the room, looking for him.

A familiar cool breeze whips around us, immediately sending a surge of adrenaline through my body. I have to stay ready to fight and manage to get up, taking Candice in my arms. The pain in my ribs is still making it hard to get a full breath but I keep trying because the room is starting to spin. I can't leave her alone.

Mrs. Stephens is walking the perimeter of the room, repeating her words as she tips the vile, allowing the black water to drop on the floor. Without warning, what sounds like hundreds of voices fill up the room, making it impossible to hear, while millions of black, dust-like specs swirl around the room.

My eyes are drawn up when I realize the black shadow creatures are back, turning in circles above our heads. Bloodcurdling screams and horrific, demonic cries reverberate around us as if they're having a war with one another. Shrieks fade in and out until every last creature finally vanishes into midair, silent. I shift my eyes back and forth, looking for Atticus, but there's no sign of him.

I don't know what the hell Mrs. Stephens is doing, but it's working. She's shouting her words, chanting them louder and louder, shaking the vile of black liquid in the air. I can actually feel the negativity being forced out of the room. The room is still smoky but it feels lighter somehow—even though it's nighttime, it's not as dark as it usually is. Like a million pounds of heavy steel has been lifted from the entire house.

I'm still holding Candice close me, hoping she stays still and doesn't fight anymore. When I feel her arm around my waist, I look down to see two amazing blue eyes smiling up at me. She's back.

"Candice," I whisper and kiss the top of her head. "You okay?" I wonder if she remembers any of this.

"I think so." She touches her temple. "My headache is gone."

Feeling a tap on my shoulder, I look to my right and see Mrs. Stephens. The serious expression on her face makes me cautious all over again and I stiffen up, hoping the worst is over.

Her face changes, as if she's just now feeling the weight has lifted, and she smiles, still holding the vile of black liquid. "It's time to leave."

"Yeah," I answer, hanging on to Candice for support because she's now become my crutch.

Candice and I walk through the window before Mrs. Stephens and when I stop to look back, she turns around and faces the window. Why is she turning back?

"Mrs. Stephens?" I call to her. "Are you coming?" I ask, hoping like hell shit isn't starting up again.

She turns back to me and winks, as if she knows I'm starting to worry, then pulls something out of her bag. She shows us a small, white bottle and we watch as she pours a little of the liquid into her palm and then sets her purse down. She rubs both hands together as she makes the sign of the cross above, below, and on each side of the window. She bows her head for a couple of seconds before she turns back around to face us.

"Okay, it's sealed," she says, dropping the bottle back in her bag. "Let's go."

I'm able to finally get a full breath because the air is better outside, though it hurts like a mother. I can't help swearing at the pain.

Mrs. Stephens looks at me like she's seeing my wounds for the first time. "I'm taking you straight to the hospital," she says, giving me a concerned, motherly kind of look.

I'm in no shape to argue, much less drive, and the thought of a hospital dosing me up with pain medicine is starting to sound like an excellent idea.

"Okay," I say as she opens her passenger door. Clenching my teeth, I hunch down to get in the seat, trying not to cry out. Candice holds on to my right arm, allowing me to use her weight, and I close my eyes, trying to ride out the agony shooting in my ribs.

"You better make it quick," Candice says to Mrs. Stephens from the back seat.

The ride is excruciating but we make it pretty quickly. Once we're at the emergency doors, Mrs. Stephens throws her Volvo into park, telling us to wait until she can get some help.

I'm half sitting, half lying down when I hear Candice pull herself up, away from me. My eyes are closed but I can tell she wants to say something when she touches my shoulder. "I'm so sorry, Brad. I'm so very sorry..." She starts to cry but I'm too tired to even talk. I manage to shake my head, hoping she knows I don't blame her.

The next thing I know, two men wearing blue scrubs are pushing me on a gurney through the hospital's double doors.

CHAPTER TWENTY-EIGHT
~ ~ CANDICE ~ ~

MRS. STEPHENS CALLED Brad's parents immediately after he was admitted, telling them what
happened and to come to the hospital as soon as
possible. I stood next to her at the pay phone, listening to
her story, nervous and shaking and out of my mind with
worry for him all at once. She glanced over at me for a split
second and rubbed my arm as if she knew I was consumed
with guilt. Then she cleared her throat and continued, telling Brad's parents that we'd been investigating the Emory
house for a class project at school. She paused, I assume
to listen to their concerns, before agreeing it was a really
bad idea that we snuck into an abandoned house. She ef-
fortlessly described how Brad "lost his balance" at the top
of the already dilapidated stairs. Fortunately, she was very
convincing and never gave out too many details. Apparently, when parents find out their kids are hurt, how it happened isn't all that important. And the fact that she's an
adult who works at the school definitely gave the story cred-

ibility. Obviously, she couldn't tell them the real truth, that a deranged ghost attacked Brad when he interfered in my assisted attempt to commit suicide. Nobody would believe that. I shudder just thinking about it.

I'm just thankful Atticus is gone, though I'm surprised I'm not even a little sad about it. He was a strange addiction—I thought I truly wanted to stay with him forever. But none of it was real. He was the one driving my feelings and once I walked out of that house for the last time I felt nothing at all. It was like Mrs. Stephens did her magic and my brain had been given back to me.

I can't help wondering what happened to him. Where does someone that evil go?

After Mrs. Stephens hangs up with Brad's parents, I begin shooting off question after question, my words running into each other in my need to get them out. She places her finger to her mouth, clearly wanting me to keep my voice down.

Scanning the area, she takes my hand and guides me to a set of chairs in a corner. "Sit down and breathe, honey," she says. "It's been a day."

I nod, taking a few deep breaths. I'm physically exhausted but somehow my thoughts are spinning out of control. I need to process the insanity of the afternoon.

Mrs. Stephens leans a little closer to me, so she can talk softly. "Okay." She rubs my arm, still completely composed and I'm grateful for it because it's keeping me calm. "What would you like to know?"

I'm so antsy, I barely give her time to finish her last words. "How could this have happened? How could a ghost be so freaking powerful?" I ask, trying to push back this new feeling of anger welling up inside me.

"First of all, we need to back up a bit," she says. "You see, Atticus was stuck in the house for nearly a hundred years."

"Okay, I get that," I interrupt. "So what? He sits around all day and practices his abilities?"

Her brows go up like she's agreeing with me in her mind. "Well, yeah, sort of." She looks down the hall and back to me. "After that much time, his deep loneliness manifested into anger and resentment, which in turn, kept him trapped. Pure and simple. Even if it was his own doing."

"Are you saying he gained that much power from being pissed and lonely?"

She laughs and nods her head so apparently, I'm finally catching on. "Pretty much. That's what created those horrible shadow creatures. As you now know, he had decades to master his abilities. When someone dies the way he did they're more likely to become trapped by their own fears. He clearly didn't think it through, we already know that, and I have no doubt his mental state was questionable. His suicide was a direct result of Josephine's death. When she passed away, he basically lost his mind over it and thought the only way he could be with her was to die himself. Unfortunately for him, Josephine's spirit moved on. His did not."

It's still hard for me to wrap my brain around that one. I don't ask about the whole spirit moving on thing, or why she—I mean, I—waited so long to come back to him. It's a little too insane to think about, but everything she said makes sense.

I could sense bits and pieces of his thoughts and emotions when Atticus was in my head. Mrs. Stephens is right, in his warped mind he never thought he could leave that house and go wherever people go when they die. Suicide was against everything he was taught and he had truly convinced himself that going to Hell was his only option. But it's hard to believe he was so distraught over Josephine's death that he didn't even consider it beforehand. He really must have been out of his mind and I have no doubt that he stayed that way all these years.

Mrs. Stephens smiles but I can tell there's concern underneath, "I know it's a lot to take in. Heck, it's a lot for me to take in and I've been doing this for years."

I tilt my head because she's piqued my curiosity. "You've done stuff like this before?"

Her face changes, blooming with pride, and I instantly realize this is an important part of her life. "Every encounter is different but yes, I have."

"You must have some crazy stories."

She looks me for a few seconds, like she's mulling her thoughts over in her head before deciding how much to say. "I was eight years old when I noticed I could see things that other people couldn't," she begins. "In my family, it was totally normal, although it skipped a generation. My mother had a hard time understanding me." She looks away as if recalling some painful memories then smiles. "Thankfully, my grandmother had the gift too, and when I was thirteen, I moved in with her and my grandpa. She taught me everything I know."

"That must have been hard," I say, watching as little wrinkles form in the corner of her eyes.

"It was. At thirteen, I was already a mess from being a typical teenager. But I was used to chaos. Well, spiritual chaos, that is. When my grandmother took me in, my life changed for the better."

"You say she taught you everything you know. What do you mean? Did you sit around a Ouija board or something?"

Her eyes go wide and she grabs my hand. "God no!" She scans the hallway as if she's afraid she spoke too loudly. "And don't ever mess with those."

"Why?"

"Because, even though they look like a board game, they're not. They actually work. Sure, they can channel spirits of dead relatives, but they can also channel really nasty ones, too.

"Is that something your grandmother taught you?"

"Among many other things, yes, and it's also why I understand Atticus like I do.

"Is she still alive?" I ask, hoping I'm not asking something too personal.

Mrs. Stephens's face drops a little and I know she's not. I place my hand on hers. "Thank her for me. Will ya?"

She smiles, a little surprised and says, "You already did."

An overhead speaker goes off, paging one of the doctors, and we both look up.

"Come on," Mrs. Stephens says, pulling me out of my thoughts. "How's your ankle?"

"Oh," I say, looking down. I'd forgotten about my ankle. I wiggle it experimentally. "It hurts a little, but not nearly like it did."

"Good." She smiles. "Let's go check on your mom."

~~

When we stop at the front desk of the ICU to check in, the nurse asks us to wait for Dr. Calloway. Apparently, something new has developed with my mom and he wants to talk to me about it. To say I'm nervous would be an understatement. I'm sure she's gotten worse. I'll be an orphan by tomorrow, I just know it.

Five minutes later he walks out of the double doors and sits down across from us. He looks at me, then to Mrs. Stephens, asking permission to talk freely in front of her. I tell him it's okay and he scratches his head like he's confused.

"I'm not sure how to tell you this, but..." He pauses, looking down at his clipboard as Mrs. Stephens takes my hand.

Doctor Calloway looks back up at me and says, "Thirty minutes ago, your mother woke up from her coma." His brows push together like he's still in disbelief but then a smile slowly washes over his face.

Mrs. Stephens instantly gives me a hug and whispers, "She's free of him, too."

I smile back at her, wiping a tear from my cheek, and try to listen to everything Dr. Calloway says.

He admits that he's amazed by Mom's progress and that it's nothing short of a miracle because only hours before, he didn't have much hope for her. When she came out of the coma and began talking to the nurse in her room, nobody could believe it. They called Dr. Calloway, who immediately checked on her, and sure enough, her brain was functioning normally again.

He did warn me that head injuries are tricky and they still needed to do more tests, but for the most part, he thinks she'll be okay.

Okay. She's going to be okay.

Mrs. Stephens hands me a tissue and takes one for herself.

"Can I see her?"

"Of course!" He smiles. "She's sleeping but you can go in for a few minutes."

I smile back and nod. "Thank you, Dr. Calloway. For everything."

"I think you're thanking the wrong person." He points up, still grinning. His pager goes off and he looks at it before pushing the button to stop the buzzing. "They need me downstairs, but let the nurses know if you have more questions," he says, waving before he heads to the elevator.

Mrs. Stephens and I look at each other and she says, "Go on. I'll wait for you." she smiles and I take her hand, genuinely grateful for everything she did for Brad and me.

"I don't know what would have happened had you not shown up," I whisper as fresh tears stream down my face.

"Shh! Enough of that—my makeup's a mess already." She hands me another tissue. "Now, go see your mother," she says, practically shooing me away.

It's the same ICU nurse from earlier. She recognizes me and nods her head as I walk down the sterile hallway to Mom's room. Again, it's so quiet it almost feels like I'm invading the peaceful atmosphere. Nerves begin to prick at my stomach as I open her door but I'm relieved to see she's awake. She looks over at me and reaches out her hand. It's warm and her grip somehow settles me down inside.

She looks human again; the thick, bloody bandages are no longer wrapped around her head.

"Hi sweetie," she whispers.

"Hi." I have to catch my breath. It's been a long time since she's called me that. "I didn't think you were..." I stop myself. I'm not sure if she knows how bad her injuries were. I smile. "You look tons better."

"That's good. I was hoping I look better than I feel." She tries to laugh but coughs instead.

"You were in a pretty bad car accident, Mom. It's understandable. You'll probably have to stay for a few more days so they can make sure you're okay." I squeeze her hand. "But after that, you can come home."

"That's what they keep telling me." She goes quiet, like she's thinking about something. "I don't remember what happened. I only recall being really angry. Like in a rage, and I don't even know why."

I know why but I can't tell her.

"It doesn't matter now. The good thing is, Dr. Calloway says you're going to be okay," I say, smiling down at her. She pulls my hand toward her and I give her a hug.

"Candice?" I pull back; her eyes are somehow softer now. "Never again," she says. "Never."

I cock my head because I'm not sure what she means.

Tears begin to well up in her eyes. As if she knows I'm confused, she says, "Never again am I taking another drink."

The feeling it gives me to see her this vulnerable, this honest, overwhelms me and I lean back down to hug her again. "I'm so happy to hear that," I whisper.

The door opens and we both look up. The nurse stops in the doorway, telling me I need to let Mom rest. So I kiss her on the forehead and promise to be back in an hour or so. I slowly walk down the quiet hallway, sighing. My heart isn't pounding anymore. My legs aren't shaking. It feels like the weight of the entire world has been lifted from my body. I don't have to be on guard. I don't have to worry what's around the corner. I can freely take a deep breath. I'm suddenly grateful for this place and the smell of rubbing alcohol. Mom and I are finally free of Atticus and Brad's going to be okay, too.

Thank God for that.

After they took like a gazillion x-rays, his doctor said he cracked one rib and broke two. His head wasn't as bad as it looked, but he did need seven stitches. He has a concussion so they've sedated him for the pain and he's resting now. I don't ever want to see anyone in that much pain again. I can't deny it gnaws at my stomach that he's lying in a hospital bed because of me. Hell, two people are in the hospital because of me. As relieved as I am, I'm still angry at myself for the irrational choices I made that lead to their involvement. I should have just walked away on that first day. Why didn't I listen to my instincts?

Guilt begins blanketing my thoughts, chasing away the blissful feeling of liberation. I'm stewing in my own self-hatred when Mrs. Stephens asks if I want something to drink. It sounds good and I'll do anything to help escape my thoughts for a few minutes. Taking the elevator down to the cafeteria, we find a table next to the vending machines and she offers to buy me a cup of coffee. I say yes, though I would've preferred hot chocolate. Unfortunately, when we walked in, the cocoa machine had an "out of order" sign taped to the front.

Mrs. Stephens starts the first cup and the heavy smell of coffee hits the air. A couple minutes later, she walks back and places two cups on the table before pulling out a chair.

"Thanks," I say, taking a sip. She laughs when I make a face. It's the crappiest cup of anything I've ever had.

"Yeah, it's pretty bad," she admits, pushing her cup away. Then she cocks her head as if she's sensing my emotions.

And she probably is. I'm getting used to it, I think, her reading me.

"Well, at this rate, the hospital should probably set you up a cot." She laughs, trying to lighten my mood.

I'm sure she knows I feel like shit for putting her and Brad through hell. I take another sip, glad it tastes terrible. It's exactly what I deserve.

Mrs. Stephens reaches for my hand across the table and I look up to see the kindness in her eyes. I try not to lose it and bawl my eyes out again, so I look away.

She squeezes tighter. "You've got to stop beating yourself up about this, Candice."

"I can't help it," I whisper, wiping a tear with my thumb.

"Sweetheart, you need to look at what you still have: a mother who's miraculously improving and a boyfriend who's going to be okay."

I immediately look up at her when she mentions the word "boyfriend" and smile. Boyfriend.

I could get used to that.

She laughs a little. "You think I don't know how you feel?"

I shake my head and close my eyes. "I just hope he feels the same after, well, you know."

"Trust me, honey, he's crazy about you. And that's not going to change."

"Oh, so now you can predict the future?" I joke, hoping she knows I'm only kidding.

"Nope, just stating a fact." She pauses to look at her watch. "We should probably get back upstairs before Brad's parents arrive. I'm sure they'll have more questions."

"Yeah, I noticed you were pretty quick on your feet."

"If you only knew, honey. If you only knew." She winks, scooting back in her chair.

I take her cue and we walk side by side to the elevator. It dings immediately and once we're inside, I remember something I wanted to ask her.

"So, what was that stuff you used?" I pause, not really wanting to say his name out loud. "You know, to get rid of him?"

"I used a few things. Which one are you talking about?"

"Can you tell me about all of them?"

"Oh, well sure. First, I cleansed the room with white sage." She watches my expression because I think she knows a lot of what happened is still foggy to me. "It was the smoky stuff."

"Oh, yeah." I remember the smoky stuff. I expected it to smell bad and it didn't. "What was the black liquid stuff?"

"Tar Water," she says, reaching in her bag. She pulls a fresh vial thing out of her purse, holding it with the tip of her fingers to give me a better look. It's brownish-black and seems to be slightly thicker than regular water. When she pulls off the top to give me a better look, I dip down and the odor instantly causes my nose to scrunch up. It smells like exactly like actual tar, like they use to black top roads.

"What does it do?" I tilt my head, watching her put the top back on.

"It's one of the only things that can get rid of extremely strong spirits. And let me tell ya, Atticus was more powerful than any other spirit I've ever dealt with," she admits, placing the vial back in her bag. "That's why I brought extra."

"Do you think it worked?" I ask, hoping her answer is yes.

"I think so. I mean, at the time, my main goal was just to get you guys out of there in one piece." She begins rubbing her fingers as if she's thinking and says, "As far as I know, he's gone. I didn't feel him in the house when we finally got out of there."

"And thank goodness for that," I say, looking down when the elevator chimes and the doors open.

"Yes. So let's stop worrying about him and start thinking positively. He's gone and that's all there is to it." She rubs her hands together and winks. "Now, I have to get some paperwork from the doctor so you'll be excused for a few days and then I'm going home. I can come back if you need me."

"Oh, no...go home to your family. I'll be fine." I stop, and the second I do, she hugs me. I think we're both fighting back tears.

"I mean it," she says. "If you need me for anything, all you have to do is call." she pulls out a piece of paper and hands it to me. I already know it's her phone number so I don't have to unfold it.

"I'm pretty sure just saying thank you isn't near enough, but it's all I know to say right now," I admit.

"You don't have to thank me, just take care of the two people in this world who need you the most." She starts to walk away then turns back to me. "And seriously, I wish you'd stop with the guilt. I can feel it all the way down the hall."

I laugh and so does she. I know she's probably right but that part is going to take me some time.

CHAPTER TWENTY-NINE

BRAD SUCKS IN a breath when the nurse yanks his arm to strap on the blood pressure cuff. Several layers of white compression bandages are around his ribs and I'm having a hard time believing she didn't notice. I give her a concerned glare. She looks at me then back to Brad. Apparently she finally realized she's been a little aggressive and apologizes, releasing his arm.

Clearly, Brad's unscathed because he immediately reaches for my hand. I'm about to get on my knees and beg his forgiveness for putting him here in the first place when there's a knock on the door and we both look up.

Two people walk in and it only takes one second for me to realize they're Brad's parents. The concerned looks on their faces pull at my heart. His mother instantly rushes over to him, gliding her palm over his face. Brad's dad follows her, standing behind, as if allowing his wife to have the first moment with their son.

"Baby," is the only thing Mrs. Davis gets out before she starts to cry.

"I'm okay, Mom," Brad tries to reassure her. "Don't cry."

"Well, this'll teach you not to sneak into old houses, son," Brad's dad says, half smiling. I think he's trying to lighten the mood, but I see him wipe a tear away.

Brad smiles, shaking his head. "Yeah, that's never gonna happen again. Oh, and sorry I had to leave the Porsche there." He looks at his father like he expects him be angry about it, then looks over to me. "You aren't going to that crazy house anymore either, right?

"Oh." He caught me off guard. "No, of course not," I say, looking up at his mom and dad, hoping they don't want to strangle me right here, right now.

Brad's mom continues to kiss and hug him and I'm starting to feel a little weird being in the room during this intimate time. Maybe even a little jealous of their bond, which is beyond screwed up.

"I should probably go so you guys can have some private time," I say, getting up from my seat.

"Oh, I'm so sorry, honey," Brad's mom instantly chimes in. "Where are my manners? I'm Doris and this is Jason." She tilts her head toward her husband and pauses, as if remembering something. "How's your mother?"

Her concern surprises me and I'm suddenly nervous. I thought she would hate me for being involved in her son's accident. Maybe even blame me. And she probably would if she knew the truth.

"Oh, she's getting much better, thank you," I answer, trying to keep myself from talking too much. "I just spoke with her doctor."

Brad's mom smiles, and the second she does, the resemblance is uncanny. I see so many of Brad's features looking back at me. She reaches out, touching my arm. "That's great news, sweetheart. The offer still stands if you'd like to stay at our house while your mother recovers."

Her sincerity is genuine; the knot in my throat just got bigger. I didn't expect this and I didn't expect her to be so freaking kind. My throat is suddenly dry when I look into her eyes.

"Oh, no, that's okay, but thank you," I manage to say without my voice cracking. I'm trying like hell to stop the tears from welling up and turn to make my second attempt at leaving. I stop when I hear Brad call my name and I look over at him.

He reaches out and says, "Please stay." The sadness behind his eyes hurts almost more than the pain I can't stand to see him in. So, without saying a word, I walk over to the chair next to his bed and take a seat. Brad holds out his hand to me and I take it, lacing his fingers in mine.

His parents must have taken that as their cue because his mom says, "We need to talk to your doctor anyway. We'll be back soon, honey." She leans over and kisses Brad's cheek, picking up her purse as she and his father walk out of the room.

The coast is clear, at least for now. This is the first time we've been alone since leaving the house. I stay silent, waiting for him to start the conversation, wondering if he wants to talk about it.

"You okay?" he asks as his brows push together.

"Yeah, but I wasn't the one who was hurt," I say, tightening my grip.

He turns his neck, cocking his head as if he's trying to get a better look at me, and says, "Let me see your neck."

"I'm fine. Really, I—"

"Candice," he interrupts me, "you may be shitty at tying a noose—thank God—but you fell pretty hard. Let me see it."

Exhaling a deep breath, because I can't let him think he can boss me around, I let go of his hand and pull my hair to one side, watching him study the rope burn just below my left ear. His fingers trace the mark ever so gently as chills begin to race down my arm.

"Not too bad, but it's still pretty red. Did anyone look at it?" he asks.

I release my hair, making sure it's covering the spot again. "No, and it's fine. Besides, how would I explain a rope burn on my neck?"

"Okay, I guess you're right," he says, agreeing with me for the first time. "What about your ankle?"

"It's fine. Now stop worrying about me." I smile, hoping to reassure him that I really am okay.

"Candice," he says softly, running his hand up my arm, "I don't blame you. None of this is your fault." He shakes his head when I look to the floor. "There was a ghost. A ghost. And he was somehow controlling you. He did this. Not you."

I look up, his words melting away some of the guilt. "So you don't hate me?" I whisper. "For dragging you into this crazy mess?"

"Of course I don't hate you! I…" The concern on his face shifts as if he wants to ask me a question, but he's not sure how. I can tell he's apprehensive about it when he blurts out, "Did you mean it?"

I know exactly what he's talking about but I'm not sure I'm ready to discuss this right now.

"Mean what?" I ask, pissed at myself for lying.

He looks down and I can almost feel his disappointment. I hate myself for upsetting him.

"Never mind," he says, taking his hand away from mine. "You were probably out of it, anyway."

Brad's right, I was out of it most of the time. But I remember pieces of it—even what I said to Atticus before nearly hanging myself. I was trying to protect Brad when I blurted it out, but when the words flew from of my mouth I knew right then they were true. I do love him, but I'm scared. Scared it'll all go away. Like everything else does in my life. Hurting him is the last thing I want, but I'm not sure what to say. I finally look up, realizing his face is turned away. "I can go if you want to sleep or something," I whisper.

He turns to face me again and I can tell he's upset. "No, I don't want to sleep. I want to talk about this," he says, adjusting his weight toward me, wincing the second he moves.

"Careful." I reach out to help, trying to get him to stop moving.

It feels like I'm about to explode from remorse. I hurt him. It's my fault he has stitches in his head and broken ribs and can't move without wincing. Every time I look at him, I'm reminded of the pain I've caused. I can't take any more lies; I have to tell him the truth. I have to so I can relieve this festering regret.

I stand up and lean in close, taking his face between my hands, and as he looks up at me with his amazing brown eyes I say, "I said it to help you. To protect you. It was a knee-jerk reaction and it worked because I think he would have killed you if I hadn't."

The compassion behind Brad's eyes says more than words. I can't hold back any longer. He deserves the truth. He deserves to know how I feel. But then he says something that changes my view on everything.

"You saved me."

I cock my head in disbelief. If anyone did any saving it was him, not me. "No, you saved me," I say. "Not only from Atticus, but from myself." Warm tears drop from my eyes. He's wiping them away as quickly as his thumbs can catch them.

"How did I do that?" he whispers.

"You kept fighting for me. And you made me believe I deserved it." I drop my face into his shoulder because I don't want him to see my face when I ugly cry. He cradles my head as my tears make a wet mess on his shoulder. I want to tell him what I started to say so I lift my head and stare back into his amazing brown eyes.

"And yes." I pause, smiling down at him. "I do love you," I whisper, tilting my head as I gently press my lips on his.

It starts out slow and sweet but then he puts his arm around my shoulders and I'm not sure if he pulls me on top or I climb in. All I know is when he moans, and it sends a sexual surge pulsating throughout my body.

It's so incredibly strong that if he weren't lying in a hospital bed at this very moment, I think I might actually consider losing my virginity. His lips taste so good and the fact that I can't touch him the way I want makes it even harder to stop. He suddenly pulls away and I open my eyes, reeling from the hormones raging through my body.

"We have to stop." He pauses, running his hand in my hair. "I want to keep going, trust me, but I'm not ready for the whole world to know how turned on I am."

"Oh, sorry." I try not to look down but it's too late. I can see exactly what he's talking about, as hospital gowns are quite thin. I can feel my face turning red as I pull my body away from him.

"Don't be. That was probably the most amazing kiss I've ever had." He takes my hand again. "And the second I get out of here, I'm gonna want to do it again." He winks then winces in pain because my eye roll made him laugh.

"Don't do that," he says, "it's too freaking painful."

Of course, we both start laughing, making him do it all over again.

A quick knock on the door catches our attention and I jump up, trying to find a blanket—anything—to put over him, but Brad is quicker, yanking a box of Kleenex from the rolling tray and placing it over his lap. I know it was probably excruciating for him reach it and I almost laugh out loud again.

Brad's mom walks back in to room with a bright smile. "We spoke to your doctor. They're keeping you for a couple of days to monitor your concussion. After

that, you can come home." Her enthusiasm is contagious and I'm smiling before she looks at me.

"Here, honey." Doris hands me a cup. "Mrs. Stephens wanted me to give you this before she left."

"Oh, thank you," I say, letting go of Brad's hand as
I reach over. I pull back the small plastic flap on the lid
and take a sip, tasting warm chocolate, and I'm thankful for Mrs. Stephens all over again.

I'm lightly blowing over the top of my drink when
I notice Brad looking toward the door then he glances
up at his mother.

"Where's Dad?"

"Oh, he's on his way," she says, setting her purse
on a table in the corner. "He didn't want to leave the
Porsche parked outside that old house overnight, so I
dropped him off."

Brad laughs. "He just wanted to drive it again."

"Probably," she says, rolling her eyes. "I think he
misses it."

"He doesn't have to miss it," Brad tells her. "He can
drive it whenever he wants."

Brad's mom laughs, reaching for something in her
purse. "Oh no, he's a man of his word." She puts a piece
of gum in her mouth. "As much as I was against it, he
gave you that car fair and square."

Brad shakes his head. "Just tell him he can drive it,
Mom. That's just silly."

"I agree, but you know your father. Once he said his
goodbyes it was officially yours." She glances over at me
then back to Brad and grins. "Although, the doctor did
say you couldn't drive for four weeks."

Brad's face instantly drops. "What? Are you serious?"

"Yes, honey. You have a concussion, remember?"

He leans his head back, running a hand through his hair. "Well, that totally sucks." He sighs. "Dad won't need an excuse now."

He looks over at me and smiles. "Need a walking buddy?"

The three of us burst out laughing.

"Don't make me laugh!" he says, folding his hands over his midsection. "I'm dyin' over here."

"You guys having a party in here?" Brad's dad says as he comes in the door. "What's so funny?"

Brad's mom giggles, reaching over to give her husband a kiss. "Yeah, you just crashed it."

I watch Brad's dad step to the other side of the bed. He touches Brad's arm and says, "I picked up the Porsche." He smiles when Brad looks up at him.

"Yeah, thanks. Mom mentioned it."

Brad's dad smiles and dangles the keys. "I'll keep her in the garage until you can drive again."

"Yeah, Mom mentioned that, too,"

His dad pats his shoulder then his face changes. He quickly reaches in his coat pocket, pulling out a piece of paper or maybe a picture, I can't be sure.

"I almost forgot. I found this sitting on the passenger seat." He hands it to Brad and as I get a closer look, my stomach drops.

"I figured you'd probably need it for your school project." Then he flips it over and says, "1910, wow. Where'd you get such an old picture of the house?"

Trying to stay calm, my eyes jerk over to Brad, but he's already looking at me.

We both know where it came from.

Atticus.

He's still here.

-The End-

Made in the USA
Columbia, SC
01 December 2021